Inviting the Wild

A Twist Upon a Regency Tale
Book 7

By Jude Knight

ARE YOU SIGNED UP FOR DRAGONBLADE'S BLOG?

You'll get the latest news and information on exclusive giveaways, exclusive excerpts, coming releases, sales, free books, cover reveals and more.

Check out our complete list of authors, too!

No spam, no junk. That's a promise!

Sign Up Here

www.dragonbladepublishing.com

Dearest Reader;

Thank you for your support of a small press. At Dragonblade Publishing, we strive to bring you the highest quality Historical Romance from some of the best authors in the business. Without your support, there is no 'us', so we sincerely hope you adore these stories and find some new favorite authors along the way.

Happy Reading!

CEO, Dragonblade Publishing

Ruadh Douglas doesn't want to go home. Years on the battle-fields for the glory of the king have made him more beast than man and he won't inflict his wounded mind and soul on his family. So, he wanders the streets of London, performing penance by rescuing those in need.

Rosalind Ransome is a misfit in London's ballrooms, but in visiting the sick of all classes, she has found work she loves and the chance to make a difference. When she is attacked in the streets, she is rescued by the vigilante they call the Wolf.

Rose is drawn to Ruadh when he seeks her family's help to free his ailing grandfather from a treacherous wife and servants. But is he the loving grandson? Or the wolf who patrols the streets at night?

Even as Rose discovers he is both, Ruadh realizes he must find a way to tame his anger if he hopes to win the maid.

But when Rose is in danger, Ruadh is glad he can still call on the wild.

Chapter One

THEY CAME FROM the shadows, half a dozen men in layers of dirty rags, with knives or broken planks in their hands and hunger in their eyes.

Reuben, the footman, moved in front of Rosalind Ransome and her stepsister, Pauline Turner. Harris, the groom, brushed past the sisters to join Reuben. He muttered, for their ears only, "Get back, my ladies, and if you see an opportunity, run."

Rose would have stepped up beside him, ready to fight, but Pauline grabbed her arm and pulled her back.

"We have to help them," Rose objected.

Pauline did not agree. "The biggest help we can be is to stay out of their way and to escape when we have the chance. They can make their own escape if they do not have to worry about us."

She did not say it was Rose's fault, but Rose knew. They were on London's streets in this unsavory area after dark because of her. But how could she have left the hospital earlier? Private Brown had asked for her. He had not been not expected to survive the night, and in fact, he didn't. Rose could do little but hold his hand. That helped, or so Mr. Parslow, the superintendent, believed.

When she'd agreed to sit with him, Rose had sent home the

carriage her brother had sent for her and her maid. She could not see any reason why her servants should sit up all night. That decision had brought them here, in the early hours of the morning, facing murder or worse for the sake of the clothes they stood up in and whatever price she and Pauline might fetch in the brothels. That was all the thieves would get, because neither of them was foolish enough to carry valuables on an errand into this part of town.

The footpads had still not attacked. Harris had a two-barrel pistol, which was making the footpads think twice, but Rose did not suppose it would deter them for long.

"Is it worth being shot?" Reuben was arguing, persuasively. "Harris is a good shot, so at least two of you will not survive. Just let us go our way and no one needs to be hurt."

"I am sorry, Pauline. I never meant for this to happen."

Pauline squeezed Rose's hand. "You did not ask me to bring the carriage back to get you, and you did not arrange for the carriage axle to collapse." Which it had done five streets after they drove away from the hospital and only three from the broader streets patrolled by the watch.

The footpads' leader had a counteroffer. "How 'bout you gie us all the morts' glimmers and you can go your way?"

Glimmers, Rose guessed, must be jewelry. "I am not wearing any jewelry," she told Pauline. "Are you?"

"No, and I do not have money with me, either."

I would rather die than be sold into a brothel, Rose decided. She put her hand into the pocket she wore under her gown, a slit in the side seam giving discrete access. At least Private Brown would not be disappointed when she did not return tomorrow. He had breathed his last some fifteen minutes before Pauline arrived with the carriage.

She unfolded the object she retrieved from the pocket, extracting the blade from the bone handle to give her a small but perfectly serviceable dagger. "I have this," she announced. "If I kill my sister and myself, will the clothing you can retrieve from our bodies be enough to compensate for this area being overrun with Red Breasts for the next few weeks until they find every last one of you? For we shall be missed, and my brother knows where we went."

The footpads went into a huddle, most of them still keeping an eye on their annoyingly uncooperative prey.

"I'm not sure you should have done that," said Pauline, and Harris, the groom, groaned. "Not a good idea, Lady Rose."

In the next moment, Rose found out why, as the footpads' leader shouted, "Take the skirts alive, especially the mouthy one!" Four of them hurled themselves towards poor Reuben and Harris, and two began skirting around the fight that ensued to grab Rose and Pauline.

Rose had no time to spare a glance for the servants, though she heard a shot. She was determined not to be taken. The man who attacked her jerked back, screaming imprecations, his hand spraying blood from the wound he had inflicted on himself when he grabbed her knife and not her hand. The second man took advantage of Rose's distraction to seize Pauline, who hit him with her umbrella. He grasped the umbrella and ripped it from her hands, then stumbled backward.

Rose took a moment to realize that a large someone in dark clothes and a cape had dragged the man away from Pauline and swung him headfirst into a wall. A meaty hand landing on her shoulder was her only warning that the assailant she had cut was back on the attack. Before she even had time to struggle, the caped man had punched him hard enough to hurl him backward.

One of the other footpads shouted, "It's the Wolf!" In moments, three of them were running. The two that had attacked Rose and Pauline lay where the caped man had put them. One of the servants' attackers was also down, presumably shot, but so was Harris. Reuben was picking himself up from the ground. As far as Rose could see in the poor light, he was unharmed.

She hurried to Harris, kneeling to feel for his pulse. As she did, he groaned. *Thank goodness!* He was alive. "Harris, can you hear me?" she asked.

"Lady Rose." He yelped as he rolled to get his legs under him. "Reuben, lad, a hand," he begged.

As she got up from her knees, Rose did not voice her objection to him moving. She could not examine him in the dark, and they needed to get off these streets as quickly as possible.

Harris said out loud what she had been thinking. "We need to get the ladies out of here before they come back to get their men."

The footpads! She had forgotten them. She took two steps toward the one who had been punched, and who was now groaning. The man they called the Wolf stopped her. "Stay back! If he can, he will use you as a shield, and your servants' suffering will be for nothing."

Oh dear. "But they have been hurt," she pointed out. "I do not like to just leave them."

"We shall leave them to their own kind," Pauline decided. "We cannot risk Harris and Reuben for the sake of men who would have killed us or sold us without a second thought. Come along, Rose."

"You are right," Rose agreed, falling obediently into step with her sister. Reuben came behind, one arm around Harris to support him. The Wolf ranged around them, sometimes ahead, sometimes behind, and sometimes walking beside them for a few paces.

In the moonlight, filtered as it was through London's fog, she could not see more of him than she had from the beginning. A large man, broad and tall. Dark clothes covered by a thigh-length cape, perhaps a domino. Try as she might, she could not see his face, even when he turned toward her to deliver a disparaging remark. He had an arsenal of them.

"This is no place for ladies of your kind."

"What would your family do if you were killed?"

"I cannot always be here to stop you from being hurt."

"You put your servants at risk. Did you think of that before you planned your little jaunt?"

All said in the accents of a gentleman and in a pleasant voice that sounded as if he might sing tenor.

The last remark was too much for Reuben, who protested, "We would not have walked if the carriage had not broken down."

RUADH DOUGLAS WAS struggling with the aftermath of battle, even more than usual. When he saw the disabled carriage, he recognized a trick Barding's gang had used before. Take out a wheel at this time of night, and the carriage was theirs. The passengers, too, whether they walked away or stayed put.

If the passengers left the carriage, the gang would pick them off first, then attack the carriage and clean it out. If they stayed, then the one attack would be enough. Ruadh had gone immediately after the passengers, hoping he wasn't too late.

He'd rounded the corner and saw Barding and his men assault the small group of naive fools. And he saw the little Amazon taking a slash at a man twice her size while her female companion thrashed another man with, of all things, an umbrella.

It looked as if the umbrella lady needed him first, but he had underestimated the resilience of the devil who had attacked the Amazon. His anger at himself as well as at Barding's insolence fueled his punch.

The others, except the one Harris had shot, ran off. They'd come back to collect their wounded, which was part of the reason Ruadh was annoyed. He should be dragging Barding to the constables, not nursemaiding this set of aristocratic idiots out of danger.

"The breakdown was no mistake," he explained to the footman who had nearly got himself killed because two fine ladies decided to go for a carriage ride through the rookeries. "Wherever you stopped tonight, you gave Barding's men the chance to damage either the wheel or the axle so you would be forced to walk."

"It must have been while we were in the hospital," the umbrella lady said. "One of my sister's patients died tonight, Mr. Wolf, or whatever your name is. He asked her to stay and hold his hand. He died shortly after midnight."

"And you nearly died shortly after that," retorted Ruadh, unreasonably irritated by the idea that the Amazon had held anyone's hand. *Except mine.* No. It was just the hot blood from battle confusing his brain. The Amazon—the man Harris had called her "Lady Rose"—was not going to be holding his hand or any other part of his anatomy.

"What hospital?" he asked, more to distract himself than because he wanted to know.

"The Hospital of St. George and St. Michael," Lady Rose replied.

Ruadh had heard of it, though it was just outside what he thought of as his patch. Outside of Barding's usual patch, too. That might be his fault. He had been pressing the Barding gang hard lately and had landed several of them in the courts and a couple in the Thames.

Barding might have thought it politic to move his operations, but he hadn't been bright enough to leave his victims alone when they chose to walk into the area that Ruadh kept safe.

They had nearly reached the first of the streets lit by gaslight and patrolled by the Watch. Ruadh caught up with the two servants and handed the footman the gun he had picked up. "Here is your friend's gun. You should be safe from here. Stop the first watchman you see and tell them what happened."

The footman nodded. Harris was wilting, but still game to walk a bit farther. Ruadh hoped he would take no permanent harm from tonight's adventure. He stopped, and the two ladies passed him. They said, in chorus, "Thank you, Mr. Wolf."

"Don't stay at this hospital at night," he growled. "Or, if you must, stay there all night until morning makes these streets a little safer. And do not ever, ever, walk them alone." He glared at Lady Rose in particular. The thought of her suffering what he'd seen in all his years in the army had added new fuel to his ever-present anger.

"I do not," she protested, and then, more softly, as if she heard the pain that made his voice harsh, "I will not, Mr. Wolf. Thank you. Mr. Wolf? Would you mind checking our carriage? I am worried about the two men we left there."

She was unusual for a lady of her obvious class. Brave, sensible—except for being in the rookeries in the first place, and unusually concerned about her servants. "I will," he promised.

They stepped out into the lighted street, and he retreated to guard them from the shadows until they found a pair of patrolling watchmen and he could be sure they were safe.

As he expected, Barding and the other two had gone by the time Ruadh got back to the place they'd fought. He checked on Lady Rose's carriage. It should be safe enough with Barding out of action and short a couple of men, but if it had been attacked, he might have been able to make a difference.

The vehicle was still where the ladies had left it, the driver alert on the carriage roof with a rifle, and the four horses sleeping in the traces. Ruadh didn't see a second man. Perhaps he had gone for help.

Ruadh resumed his patrol. He intervened in two scuffles. He forced a fop who had stopped for a quick one on his way home from some society event to pay the pleasure girl he had just tupped. He finished the night, as dawn rose, with a satisfying fight with some street tough who was beating a boy for failing to steal enough during the night hours.

"If you want a better job than this," he told the boy, after the tough was down and not getting back up, "go to the address I will give you and tell them the Wolf sent you."

The boy repeated the address and then backed away. "Be'er get the sawbones there to take a look at yer h'arm, Wolf. It's bleedin' somefink awful." He took off and was soon out of sight.

Ruadh hadn't felt the sting of the cut, but his arm hurt now the boy had called attention to it, and his sleeve was stiff with dried blood. Just as well the night was over. Getting to the free clinic whose physicians he trusted would be challenging if he lost much more blood, impossible if anyone saw fit to attack him.

He removed his cape and the red mask he wore beneath his hood and stuffed them both into the satchel he carried. His weapons were already concealed. With luck, anyone who saw him would think he was just another partygoer heading home.

He passed the place where Lady Rose's carriage had been. All was well that ended well.

PETER WAS AWAKE and waiting for Rose and Pauline. "Why are you out so late? Is everything all right?" he demanded, taking hold of Rose's shoulders, and looking her up and down.

"We are quite unhurt," Pauline told him. "Harris did not fare as well, but he insisted that it was nothing his wife could not fix. And Reuben was unharmed."

His eyes widened in alarm. "You were attacked?"

"Yes," Rose confirmed. "But we are not hurt."

"You had better tell me what happened," Peter said. He led the way to the reception room by the front door, where he must have been sitting while he waited for them. A book and a glass of brandy sat on the little table by one of the chairs, the lamp beside it casting light over the shoulder of anyone who was reading in the chair.

Rose sat in one of the other chairs and held her hands out to the warmth of the fire. She was shivering a little, though more from reaction to the danger they'd been in, and to the violence, than to the cold.

"The carriage axle broke," Pauline said. "One of the footmen went for help. We were still in the rookeries, but only a few streets away from the better-lit streets. We thought staying with the carriage would put us more at risk than making for safety."

"It was not the wrong decision, Pauline," Rose assured her. "The men who damaged the axle would have attacked the carriage if we had remained in it. Indeed, they still might have done so."

Peter, who had been pacing while Pauline and Rose talked, held up a hand. "I shall send help," he said. "The axle, you say?" He stepped out of the room and Rose could hear him talking to someone, a series of orders, by the sound. At times, Peter reverted to being the commanding officer of the cavalry he had been for so many years.

"I've sent people to retrieve the carriage," he said when he reentered the room. "Would you like a drink, Pauline?" He didn't offer one to Rose, though she was nineteen and no longer a child.

"A small brandy," Pauline agreed.

"And one for me," said Rose. Perhaps it would stop the shaking.

He was topping up his own glass from a decanter on a side table and pouring a drink for Pauline. He froze, then turned a searching look on Rose. After a moment, he picked up a third glass, put it with the others, and poured a finger of brandy into the glass.

"You were attacked, you said. And the men who attacked you said they had damaged the axle?" He passed a glass to Pauline and brought the other to Rose.

"We were attacked," Pauline confirmed. "Six men. It was going badly for us until another man intervened. The Wolf of Whitecross, Peter. Harris shot one of the men and the Wolf knocked out two others."

"It was the Wolf who told us the gang must have disabled the carriage," Rose explained. "He walked us to the streetlamps and promised to go back and check on the carriage and our men."

The Wolf of Whitecross had been in the news sheets. A shadowy figure no one but the poorest of the poor had even met. If, indeed, any of them had, for none would admit it to the watchmen or the constables. Nor could the reporters find actual eyewitnesses, only second-hand accounts of an avenging angel who stood up for the weak and the helpless. A masked angel in a cape.

"We met the Wolf," she said, in wonder.

"A man who takes the law into his own hands is not one to be admired," Peter said sternly.

"A man who saved me, Rose, Reuben, and Harris has my gratitude," Pauline retorted.

Peter sighed. "Rose, please be kind enough to tell me why you sent your maid home in your carriage and refused to come with her."

Rose had known he was going to want to know. "My patient," she explained. "He was dying, and he wanted to hold my hand. I thought I would be there all night, but he died, and then Pauline came to fetch me, so we left." She then burst into tears, to her great embarrassment.

She could not stand females who used tears to get their own way. Her stepmother, Pauline's mother, had used tears to rule the father Rose shared with Peter.

The tears refused to stop, though she tried to choke them back. Poor Private Brown. And the fate those men had intended for her! And Harris, bravely walking, with Reuben's help. There had been so much blood! Though she'd managed to bandage him with a piece of Reuben's shirt in the light of the first streetlamp they'd reached. So much blood.

Peter pulled her into a hug. "Poor Rose," he said. "It has been quite a night for you. Drink up your brandy, my dear, and then you and Pauline had better go off to bed. We shall talk some more in the morning and make a plan to keep you safe."

Peter truly was the best brother in the whole world.

"YOU CAN'T KEEP doing this, Red," said Nate Beauclair as he sewed up the gash in Ruadh's arm. "Sooner or later, one of these brutes will kill you."

Ruadh shrugged. Nate had been patching him up for four months, ever since he arrived in London with a report from the colonel of his regiment for the desk-chair officers at the Horse Guard. He hated the city. But at least here, his pain had a purpose, since it drove him out into the streets at night, where he could ease his anger, his guilt, and his despair in bursts of violence against those who deserved it.

Nate tied off the last stitch. "I mean it, Red. Go home, for your own sake, and for that of your family. I have another letter for you. I'll fetch it once I've finished bandaging this."

"I can't go home," Ruadh murmured. Heavens knew, he could not live with himself. He would not ask his family to live with him.

The doctor's hands stilled on his arm. He had been a military man himself. A sailor, not a soldier, but he, too, had seen terrible things. They had exchanged stories over a drink one cold winter's morning when the clinic was quiet and Ruadh had no place better to be. Not about the horrors of war, but just the brief outlines of where they had been and why.

The press gang had taken Nate even though he was a gentleman's son. Nate didn't explain the story behind that, but he did talk about working for the surgeon of the ship on which he found himself. He'd had a gift for it and had eventually been sent to Edinburgh to become a physician.

A medical man, so he might have seen the violence that scarred a man's soul, but he had not been the perpetrator. Rather, he was there to fix what he could, as he still did today.

A twist of fate had also made him an earl. He hadn't been born and raised to it, and he didn't go by his title here in this little clinic that offered medical care to those who otherwise would not be able to afford it.

Ruadh's story was different. He had joined the army of his own accord. Just eighteen years old, full of stories of adventure and visions of glory. The 157th Highland Foot was the regiment of his father's mother's people, including a score or more of Ruadh's cousins. Many of them died, and others broken. Some of them were sent to their deaths by his orders, along with other good men whose faces he remembered in dreams, both asleep and waking.

In the long war against Napoleon, violence was in some ways understandable, and certainly necessary. The man had to be stopped. But the ferocities of war—his own most of all—purged him of the stories and the visions and wounded something inside him. Something essential.

He'd been broken by ten years of keeping the so-called peace in the tragedy that was Ireland under English rule. In the end, his frustration with British policy in Ireland caused him to attempt to resign his commission. His colonel, also a distant cousin, would not accept it but had given him six month's leave to go home. He had got no farther than London.

He had told Nate the bare bones of the story, but the physician's wise eyes told Ruadh he understood some of the rest. The pain, if not the reasons for it.

"I can't go home," he repeated. To change the subject, he asked, "What do you know about a hospital on Little Mill Street? St. George and St. Michael?"

"A charity hospital for ex-soldiers and ex-sailors who are too injured to look after themselves but have no one else to do it for them and nowhere else to go," Nate replied. "A good place. I consult there when I am asked, but most of the residents are past any help I could give them. They need nursing, food they can stomach, and the comfort of a clean bed. Is there trouble there? Snowy and I have put the word out they are not to be touched."

Snowy was Lord Snowden, who had apparently grown up in

the rookeries. Ruadh had not met him, but he'd heard about him. "No trouble at the hospital. I rescued a lady on her way home from there. Lady Rose, her servants called her. She and her sister stayed with someone who was dying and got caught in a trap when they tried to go home while it was still night."

"Lady Rosalind Ransome, sister of the Earl of Stancroft. She's an herbalist, a protégée of Snowden's wife, who volunteers here. I heard that Lady Rosalind had taken over from Lady Snowden while she was in the country." A smile ghosted over his lips. "You would not have met Lady Snowden, for you are never here in the daytime. The other would have been the stepsister, I imagine. Miss Turner."

"Lady Rosalind called her 'Pauline'," Ruadh remembered.

Nate nodded. "That's right. Pauline Turner. They weren't hurt, were they?"

"The groom was cut, but not too badly, I think. The footman and the two ladies came out of it safely enough." He slipped off the examination bed. His head was still clear, thank goodness. He hadn't lost too much blood. "Thank you, Nate. I'm grateful."

"Don't go out for the next few nights," Nate demanded. "Give my stitches time to do their job. Oh, and Red? I've heard word that someone has hired Wakefield and Wakefield to find out who you are."

Who the hell are Wakefield and Wakefield? "Should I be worried?" Ruadh asked.

"Depends on why they are looking," Nate said. "They're good, but they're honest. When they take a case, they promise to find the truth, whether it works for their client or not. If one of the magistrates has hired them, it might be bad."

"Bounty hunters?"

"'Inquiry agents', they call themselves. Be careful, Red."

Ruadh dropped a pouch of coins on the table. "For the clinic," he said.

The physician weighed the pouch in one hand. "Somewhat more than the going rate for a physician in this part of Town," he observed.

"The rest is payment for your scolds, though I'm far past the age for a nanny," Ruadh told him. Though he teased, he appreciated what Nate had to say. Or, rather, that he cared enough to say it.

He slipped his mother's letter into his pocket as he left the clinic. He'd read it later in the little room he rented in the rookeries. Not far, as it happened, from Lady Rosalind's hospital. Perhaps he should wander by and have a look at the place.

First, though, a pie and an ale. Then a sleep—for at least as long as his dreams left him alone.

Chapter Two

A week later

M AJOR DOUGLAS WAS at the hospital again—for the third time in the five days since she'd first seen him.

Rose should not be noticing the man, let alone surreptitiously staring at him. *But, my goodness, he is hard to miss, and once seen, hard to look away from!* All that height and width, the flaming mop of red hair, and—as if that was not enough—the kilt that was part of his uniform as an officer of the Reds. The 157th (Highland) Regiment of Foot, that was. Known as 'the Reds' for the color of their kilts, the hair of so many of them, or the blood they spilled, depending on who told the story.

Rose had heard that the kilt was outlawed in the king's realms until recently, with only certain Highland regiments having a dispensation to wear it. *Heavens! If all Scots sported calves like the major's, then the prohibition was a mercy to virtuous females!*

"Rosalind?" Pauline sounded irritated. "Rose, the carriage will be ready for us."

Oh yes. They had a ball to attend tonight. Rose had better hurry up, or she would make them late, and then all three of her sisters would be annoyed with her.

"I have only one more gentleman to see, Pauline," she told

her sister. "This way." She led Pauline from the room, giving thanks that the last patient of the day was not in the same ward currently being favored by a visit from Major Douglas.

It did not take long to ascertain that Corporal Waters had benefited from the latest poultice she had created for him. "The rash ain't as hot, Miss," he told her, "and it be hardly itchy at all."

Mixing just the right ingredients in the right proportions would be easier if Rose were permitted to see the physical symptoms she was treating. Lady Snowden, her mentor, examined patients, but Lady Snowden was a married woman and a decade older than Rose. However, Lady Snowden was not here.

As a maiden of not quite twenty, Rose needed to stand at least six feet away from Corporal Waters' bed and hold a conversation about symptoms that were embarrassing to them both, particularly given the position of the rash—which she had had to deduce since the corporal had been unwilling to put it into words or even point to it.

On second thought, perhaps it was just as well that, in this instance at least, she was not permitted to see the rash for herself. "I have made up more of the mix, and have left it with the orderly," she told him.

Pauline took a pocket watch from her reticule and gave it a pointed look. Rose nodded in response. "I am coming," Rose told her and said goodbye to the corporal.

As she had expected, as soon as they were settled in the carriage, Pauline scolded her. Gently, as was Pauline's way, but a scold, nonetheless.

"Rose, darling, I could not help but notice that you were watching Major Douglas again today. Do be careful, dearest. It would be most embarrassing for you if he were to notice, or if someone else were to comment." She put her hand on Rose's arm and smiled. "A fine figure of a man, Rose. But do be careful."

Rose sighed. "I know, Pauline. I do not mean to stare. I shall try harder if we encounter him again."

What else could she say? Pauline was correct. Rose really

should not allow herself to be distracted by the gentleman. She had not even had an introduction to him and didn't expect that to change. Apart from her volunteer work as an herbalist, her life was the circumscribed one of an earl's sister.

She was unlikely to meet a Scots army major at the sort of entertainments she attended with Vivienne, her closest half-sister and dearest friend, and nothing would come of it if she did. If he was of a class to attend such affairs, he was too high-born to bother with Rose, even though she had been raised as if she was of noble—and legitimate—birth on both sides. No one was rude to her face, for fear of offending Peter, but everyone knew she was Peter's illegitimate half-sister, the daughter of their father's mistress. Most of them assumed she was destined to be a mistress herself.

It was the story of her life. Her family regarded her as a lady, the daughter of an earl, while prospective suitors heard the circumstances of her birth and turned away. She was, as her old nurse used to say of something that did not fit, neither fish, nor fowl, nor good red meat. She could not marry within her class because the base-born had no class.

Her path had almost crossed that of Major Douglas by chance at the hospital, with each of them on their own errands, and moving in different directions. That would be the end of it. In any case, the frowns Major Douglas sent her way indicated his disapproval of her presence. He was probably like so many men, determined that women of her apparent class should be decorative, agreeable, silent, and kept away from pain, suffering, and anything else that was real.

He clearly had no interest in knowing her, so these ruminations were unutterably foolish.

RUADH KEPT RETURNING to the hospital. On his first visit, he had found more than a dozen Scots veterans, all with no home to go to and nobody to care whether they lived or died. One was from his own regiment. Like all the soldiers and sailors cared for here, he had been released as unable to serve. Injuries or illness had left these Scotsmen unfit, not just for the army or the navy, but for any civilian job. Stranded hundreds of miles south of their own country, without families to take them in, they were doomed to a short life on the streets.

Each had a story of how they came to Geordie and Mick's, as they fondly called it. Some had been directed by other beggars on the street. Some had been sent by clinics such as the one at which Nate volunteered. Still others had been told of the place by vicars or kindly strangers.

"It isn't home, Major," one told him, "but it is better than the street." His eyes slid past Ruadh to the ladies who were passing down the ward toward the door. "Scenery is better, too."

The soldiers had told Ruadh that Lady Rosalind was an angel, and she certainly looked like one, with her fair hair and eyes so blue a man could drown in them.

Ruadh had no idea what her family was thinking, letting a pretty girl like her come to a place like this. When he protested to the superintendent, though, the man shrugged. "Her brother, the Earl of Stancroft, is on the board of trustees," he said, "as is Lady Snowden, her mentor. If they say she can come here with her potions and her poultices, then I cannot prevent her. Mind you," he added, as if bound and determined to be fair, even against his own prejudices, "She and Lady Snowden do the lads good. Quite apart from their concoctions, which mostly seem to work, they are a sight for sore eyes. Especially Lady Rosalind."

"Aye," Ruadh agreed, "and that is why she should not be here. These soldiers—fine lads, most of them, but rough, Mr. Parslow. You must agree they are rough. If they should offer insult to the lady, either intentionally or just because they know no better—"

Parslow interrupted. "That's just what they will not do, Major. If a man hurt a hair of her head or her least sensibility, the rest of them would have his guts out in a flash and make them into garters for their stockings. You've no need to worry that Lady Rosalind will come to any more harm here than she would in her sister-in-law's parlor."

With that, Ruadh had to be content, and after all, it was none of his business what the Earl of Stancroft allowed his sister to get up to. Not that he stopped thinking about Lady Rosalind. In Spanish, the name would be pretty rose, and it suited her. She was pretty and she had the skin of a rose. One of those soft pink roses his mother loved so much.

It would be as soft as a rose too, he would bet his last shilling, and as sweet-smelling. Not that he was expected to be able to test that supposition. In fact, his mother's news meant he wasn't going to be able to stay in London for much longer.

Duty called him north, to the last place on the planet he wanted to be. He had one more task to carry out for his mother, and perhaps one for these men and others like them. Could he set up a hospital like this for the 157th Scots Foot? Or perhaps for all the Scots regiments? Something in Glasgow or Edinburgh, perhaps, so any family they had left could visit them and so at least they could breathe Scottish air until they breathed no more. He couldn't do it on his own, of course. He would need to find sponsors.

Da might be able to help with that. If so, it would be a silver lining to his mother's unpalatable news. Ruadh's father's unexpected elevation had shocked him to the core and also made it impossible to stay away.

An obscure country scholar whose brother had done his duty and produced an heir and a spare could allow his son Ruadh to join the army, serve the Crown for his entire adult life so far, and tarry in London for the rest of it. No one but his parents would care, and if they didn't understand, they at least loved him enough to leave him be.

But as the son of the newest Earl of Glencowan, he was now

Viscount Merrick and Master of Glencowan. He found it hard to grieve the uncle he could barely remember and the cousins he'd never known. But when their yacht went down in a sudden squall, his chosen life died, too.

The void where his heart used to be howled at the thought of taking his pain home. He would have to keep busy—work had always been the only poultice for his internal wounds and that meant the constant tasks of a senior officer in the army or, more recently his self-imposed position as the Wolf of Whitecross.

Yes. A hospital might be just the thing. A task to do. One that made the world just a little better.

At that, Ruadh might see Lady Rosalind again, for he would need to call on her brother, who was chair of the Board of Trustees of Geordie and Mick, to discuss the logistics of such a venture.

Not today, though, for the hour drew late. And not tomorrow, when he had a commission to carry out for his mother.

She was worried about her father and wanted Ruadh to call on him. Ruadh supposed he ought to have done it without being asked, but he had never got on with the sour old man, who had not forgiven Da for inveigling his daughter away to the north of the border, and who tended to blame Da's children for being of Da's blood.

Still, if the old man was ill or in trouble, Mama would expect Ruadh to look after him. Mama was the kindest soul on God's earth and never held a man's sins against him when he was in need.

Perhaps the day after tomorrow, as his reward for being a good son, he might call on the Earl of Stancroft and catch a glimpse of the beautiful Rosalind.

"Good day, Lord Hardwicke," called Rose across the garden

wall. The elderly neighbor had been rolled out in his bath chair and parked on the terrace, just across the wall from the herb pots she had on the terrace of her brother's townhouse.

The gardens near the house were narrow and shaded by neighboring trees. Pauline's roses were farther down the garden and got the sun most of the day, and Rose had a patch for her herbs down there, too. The terrace was out of the shade of the trees and caught the full afternoon sun. The plants that most needed her care flourished here within a few steps of the house.

Lord Hardwicke, not so much. He looked more and more frail each time she saw him. "Lady Rose," he called. "A pleasant day for a spot of gardening."

At least, that was what she understood him to say. His speech had recovered a lot—it had been almost gone altogether after the apoplexy he had suffered a couple of months ago. It was still garbled and hard to understand.

"I am cutting back the peppermint before it runs to flower, Lord Hardwicke," she explained.

In answer to a garbled question, she agreed. "Yes, I will use it in tinctures at the hospital, to bring down fevers."

In their conversations before his apoplexy, she had learned he had a personal interest in military hospitals. His grandson was a soldier, currently stationed in Ireland with one of the Highland regiments, and Lord Hardwicke worried about him.

Poor Lord Hardwicke. He had been lonely before his apoplexy and things were worse now. Before, he had few visitors and went out seldom. Now, he went nowhere, and the trickle of visitors had dried up to nothing. Rose wondered if they had been turned away at the door, as she had been in the early days after the apoplexy, when she had become worried at his continued absence from his garden.

However, since his body failed, his wife had begun to entertain frequently. She had guests now. Rose could hear the tinkle of teacups and the buzz of conversation, drifting through the windows that were open in the heat of the day.

That was probably why the poor old man was out on the terrace. Lady Hardwicke would not want her guests to see him. That was another thing that had changed since Lord Hardwicke was struck down. Lord and Lady Hardwicke used to stay at home together, she busying herself with buying new drapes, furniture, and ornaments for the house, and he with his books and his garden.

Before, Lady Hardwicke was all sweet words and flattery. "Yes, my lord. You are so clever, my lord. It must be as you say, my lord." Not after. Rose had heard her talking to her poor husband. She obviously had not seen Rose, who was kneeling down to weed the pots, for Lady Hardwicke did not measure her words.

"You useless lump of meat. Why could you not have died in your fit? I would be a rich widow. Well. The doctor says the next one could kill you, so we live in hope, Phillip and I. I cannot wait for the day I can dance on your grave. Perhaps I won't wait. Phillip says it would be a kindness to hold a pillow over your face."

"Na i' m a will." Lord Hardwicke forced out the words, and Lady Hardwicke slapped the poor old man's face.

Phillip, Rose had discovered through the medium of the network of servants in the surrounding houses, was Phillip Wolfendale, Lord Hardwicke's valet. Rose had seen him. His hair was white, though he was at least ten years younger than Lady Hardwicke. Rose put his age in the mid-twenties.

His skin was pale, too, and his eyes were a startling pale blue. He had seen her peering over the wall, though Lady Hardwicke never noticed. Seen her and challenged her, for he had come close to the wall and stared into her eyes.

"The Ransome bastard, isn't it? Mind your own business, *Miss* Rosalind Ransome. There is nothing to interest you on this side of the wall, and people who interfere are liable to come to bad ends."

Rose still felt a shiver of fear when she remembered the look he gave her.

IT WAS THREE days after he had last seen Miss Ransome at the hospital that Ruadh was finally able to call on her brother. He had visited this street twice before in the past few days, calling on his grandfather, for the old man had a house that was not only in the same row as that occupied by Lord Stancroft and his family, but it was right next door.

Calling on, but not seeing. Both times he had given his card to the butler and announced his name and his relationship to the Earl of Hardwicke. Both times, the butler went away and came back to say that the earl was not at home, English upper-class code for not receiving—what was it his grandfather had said last time Ruadh had called?—the misbegotten whelp of that thieving Scotsman Douglas.

Third time is the charm, Ruadh figured, and this afternoon, after his call on Miss Ransome's brother, he would try again. He would then consider his mother's errand accomplished as best as he could.

Meanwhile, he put the unpleasant duty out of his mind, for he had high hopes for his visit to the Earl of Stancroft. Not only did he hope for encouragement and advice from Stancroft, who had himself once been an officer in the King's army and who was by all accounts a pleasant fellow, but if the fates were with him, he might also catch a glimpse of the lovely Lady Rosalind.

The butler greeted him with a nod and a smile. "You are expected, Lord Merrick. I am to show you in."

Ruadh followed. He had made the appointment as Major Douglas, but clearly, Stancroft had checked to find out exactly who Major Douglas was.

Stancroft was in his study, but not alone. Two ladies sat with him, and one was Lady Rosalind. The other wore an eye-catching mask that had been painted to match the embroidery on her gown and covered half her face. Ruadh had heard about Lady Stancroft's mask, so this must be her.

"Lord Merrick," said Stancroft, rising and extending his hand.

Should Ruadh challenge the use of the title? It was correct, after all, and he supposed he was going to have to get used to it. "Lord Stancroft. Thank you for making time to see me."

"Of course," the earl said. "You offer an intriguing opportunity to help spread the good work the hospital has done. I have asked my wife and sister to join me, as they are both involved with the hospital in different ways and have perspectives that may be useful to you. My love? Rose? May I present Lord Merrick, the Master of Glencowan. Merrick, Lady Stancroft, and my sister, Lady Rosalind Ransome."

Lady Stancroft smiled at him. "Stancroft and I hope we can be of assistance. One hospital cannot help all those in need, so it pleases me more than I can say to think you are interested in taking ours as inspiration. Please be seated, Lord Merrick."

Lady Rosalind was frowning at him. Was it the name?

He accepted the chair to which he was directed. "Thank you, Lady Stancroft. It is pleasant to meet you and Lady Rosalind. Stancroft, Lady Rosalind and I have seen one another at a distance several times recently when we have both been visiting the hospital. They know me as Major Douglas, there. I am more comfortable with my army rank, which I earned, than with the title I only learned about a week ago. Still, I will need to become accustomed, so let it be Lord Merrick."

He had guessed right. The little furrow between the lady's brows smoothed, and she even smiled a little.

Stancroft waved him to a chair. "It took me months to stop looking around for my father whenever I was addressed as Lord Ransome, and then I was granted the earldom, and had to get used to yet another title." He and his wife exchanged a warm look filled with an intimacy that made Ruadh both embarrassed to be a witness and envious of their love.

"The Stancroft title was originally my father's, Lord Merrick," said Lady Stancroft, "so I changed my birth surname for the title of Lady Ransome and then that title for the one I associated with my mother. One does grow accustomed."

They spoke a little more about the challenges of stepping into a predecessor's shoes and even their name, until Stancroft turned the conversation to the business that had brought Ruadh here. "I understand from your letter that you want to set up a hospital along the same lines as ours, but in Scotland to serve veterans who came from that area. And you hope to hear from us what we did and why, to help you with your project. Can you expand on that?"

Stancroft was correct about the two ladies. As the conversation progressed, they made significant contributions. Lord Stancroft talked about organization, funding, and management.

Lady Stancroft spoke from the perspective of a patient. She had been badly burned in a fire as a child—hence the mask covering half of her face—and she had spent a long time recovering. She talked about the importance of things to do that made an injured person feel useful and needed, of leisure activities to give pleasure, of someone to talk to about the experience of healing. She also explained how important it was for patients to be supported as they grieved for a life changed by an injury and encouraged and to let go of anger, impatience, and other negative emotions, and to see the promise of the future in spite of one's injury.

"We house those who will never recover more than they already have. Who will, in fact, slowly deteriorate as they age. There is grief in that, but also strength in learning to take joy in what remains."

As for Lady Rosalind, she, too, made a great deal of sense. "Our patients have had enough of doctors—and the doctors of them, I rather think. Doctors want to make people well, but they place less focus on making them comfortable. If scars are pulling, Lady Snowden and I can provide a cream that will help. If a man has lost his right hand, we can suggest he uses his left, and encourage him until he is skilled. If he has lost a great deal of weight and is feeling the cold, we can find someone to provide a blanket. You need a strong group of volunteers, Major, to provide the comforts that make life more pleasant."

She did not say, but Ruadh thought, that pretty young volunteers must be a medicine in themselves. Certainly, if he were to judge by the way the soldiers at the hospital talked about "their" Miss Rosalind, she did them good just by walking into the ward. Besides beauty, she projected a feminine serenity and peace very different from the violence and aggression men—especially soldiers—emitted. Even he found himself basking in the warmth of it, and feeling calmed, however briefly.

Ruadh was shocked when he noticed the time. "My ladies, my lord, I did not realize how much time had passed." He began to gather his notes. "This has been invaluable. I cannot begin to tell you how grateful I am."

"It has been our pleasure," Peter said, standing to hold out his hand to Major Douglas. No, she must get used to thinking of him as Lord Merrick. "Please let us know how you progress."

Lord Merrick promised he would do so.

"Are you planning to stay in London for long, Lord Merrick?" Arial asked. Rose had wanted to ask the same question. The gentleman had impressed her at first sight but hearing his errand and then talking with him about the issues had broadened her appreciation. Now, her admiration was not just for his fine looks, but for his compassion and determination. Yes, and the way he listened with respect not just to Peter's countess, but to her.

There was also something familiar about him. Some elusive memory that refused to come to the surface to be recognized. Not the golden-brown eyes that could look fierce, kind, and passionate by turns, nor the tousled red hair. But something.

"THANKS TO YOU all, Lady Stancroft," Lord Merrick replied to Arial. "I am much closer to completing one of my errands in London. I have a meeting early next week at Horse Guards to talk to Brigadier General Lord Redepenning about visiting the military hospitals."

He grimaced. "I do not expect such success with my other errand. I have been attempting to visit your neighbor, the Earl of Hardwicke, but he will not see me."

"Since his apoplexy," Rose offered, "Lord Hardwicke has not seen anyone."

Rose suddenly became the object of Lord Merrick's intent stare, and that elusive memory tickled her thoughts again. Something about him—his height, or maybe it was just that intensity in his gaze? Something…

"He has had an apoplexy? The butler just said he was not at home. I thought he was refusing me an audience. After last time…" He trailed off, frowning as if his thoughts bothered him.

He looked so troubled that Rose could not resist asking, "What is it, Lord Merrick?"

He turned that frown on her, then his face softened. "I was wondering what I am going to tell my Mama, Lady Rosalind. She will insist I see him for myself, but if they won't let me in…"

"What is Lord Hardwicke to you, my lord?" Ariel asked.

He blinked as if surprised to find the other two still with them. "My grandfather. My mother's father. She decided that something was wrong with him and asked me to check for her. My mother has what we Scots call 'a touch of the fae'." Lord Merrick shrugged. "My grandfather was not pleased that his daughter married a Scot, and especially not a younger son. When I called on him seven or eight years ago, we ended up having an argument over the way he had cast her off. However, he started writing to my mother after that, so it was worth the visit." He appeared to shake this personal history off and turned to Rose. Once again, his intense gaze stirred something deep in her memory that just wouldn't present itself. "Do you know his condition? Is he expected to make any sort of recovery?"

"You are the major who was stationed in Ireland," Rose realized. Lord Hardwicke's Ruadh, of whom he was so proud. 'Rooah', the elderly gentleman had said and then had spelled it for her, chuckling a little, perhaps over a memory he did not share.

"He used to speak of you often when he could still speak. He says you have the courage to stand up for yourself and those you love, and that you are loyal to family. You are a good soldier, too, he says. Decorated after Waterloo."

Lord Merrick flushed a little at the praise, but he nodded, decisively. "I must see him, then. Even if he does not want to see me."

"He might not know you have called," Ariel warned. "Lady Hardwicke has been turning people away."

"Lady Hardwicke," Lord Merrick repeated. "My mother said he had recently married again. A widow, I believe. Perhaps I should ask to speak with her, and explain I need to see him to satisfy my mother."

"Yes," Rose agreed. She thought of Phillip and his threat. Something should be said, she decided, but in a roundabout way. She had no doubt Lord Merrick would be able to discern there was a problem with Lord Hardwicke's treatment by his wife and her…whatever Phillip was to her. "I think that is a good idea. Perhaps—do you mind if I offer a suggestion, Lord Merrick?"

"Please. I would be grateful." He inclined his head.

"Insist, my lord. Be as polite as you wish but make it clear that his daughter is worried about her father, and if you are not permitted to see him, you will return with a magistrate."

Lord Merrick's eyes had widened at her suggestion. "Do you have reason to believe that Lady Hardwicke is hiding something, Lady Rosalind?" Good, she thought. She was not wrong about him. He understood her meaning and yet, Phillip wouldn't be able to trace her to the cause of any investigation on the part of the magistrate.

Peter spoke before Rose could. "I think you should see Lady

Hardwicke and draw your own conclusions before Rose answers that question." As usual, Peter played her protector. Such a good brother. "Go and make your visit. Observe. Come and see us tomorrow afternoon, and we shall tell you what we know. Rose is the one who is best acquainted with your grandfather, for he used to speak to her from the other side of the wall when they were both gardening."

"And I still converse with him, Peter, when they wheel him out to take the sun—" or to hide him from view—"although his speech is now very hard to understand."

Their visitor was taking it in, looking from one of them to the other. His eyes were hooded and there was a fierceness in his expression that made Rose shiver. She had watched him with his men and knew how kind he could be, but seeing him now left her in no doubt that he'd been a fierce warrior on the battlefield. *I think he is no stranger to violence when it is needed.*

"Come and see us tomorrow," Peter repeated.

Lord Merrick stood. "I will, my lord, and thank you."

Rose, her attention on Lord Merrick, crossed the room to summon the butler to show their guest out, but she tripped on the corner of a rug. She would have fallen—and fully expected to fall—but Lord Merrick must have crossed the room in a flash, for he was there to catch her and put her back on her feet.

"Thank you," she said, breathless more at his proximity and the feel of his hands, however briefly, on her waist than at her own averted accident. She could still feel the heat and strength of them even though he'd already stepped back to stand at a respectable distance.

"I am glad I was here to stop you from hurting yourself," he said, and Rose stilled, remembering very similar words in the same light tenor. A man of this height and build, too. And that intensity radiating off of him…

No, it could not be. Lord Merrick was a viscount. A major in the army. He could not also be the Wolf of Whitecross.

She looked up at him but stopped herself from staring. *Could he?*

Chapter Three

T HIS TIME, THE Hardwicke butler refused to admit him at all. "You again. My instructions are…"

He got no further, because Ruadh picked him up and walked him backward. He then put the man down and shut the front door.

He handed the open-mouthed and wide-eyed butler another of his visiting cards. Under his name and rank, which was all that was printed on the card, he had written his English and Scots titles. "If his lordship is not available, I shall see Lady Hardwicke."

The butler drew himself up, closing his mouth and recovering his dignity as he did so. "Her ladyship is not available."

Ruadh sat down on one of the upright chairs against the wall. "Then I shall wait until her ladyship is available. Inform Lady Hardwicke that I have been sent by my mother, Lord Hardwicke's daughter. She is concerned about her father and has charged me with seeing him." He didn't try to use the more cultured yet polite tone of the peerage; instead, he used his Major voice, the one that dripped with the warning of stripes and stockades if orders weren't followed.

The butler responded by thinking better of whatever he was about to say. He left the entry hall, presumably to speak to Lady Hardwicke. A moment later, a pair of footmen appeared, sized

Ruadh up with their eyes, and took up posts on either side of the front door.

Ruadh set his feet firmly and stared at them till they both looked away. *Aye, my lads. Moving me is beyond the pair of you.* Ruadh might succumb to four of them, but he could do a lot of damage before they managed to get him out of the house. Mind you, it wouldn't come to that. If Lady Hardwicke insisted he leave, he would go and put Lady Rosalind's backup plan into operation. It appeared his ministering angel wasn't wrong in her estimation that something was happening here, for why else would the lady of the house be making such strenuous attempts to keep him from visiting with his grandfather?

He might need the magistrate to visit even if he was admitted to see the man.

The butler did not return within a few minutes to deny him an audience. Ruadh took that as a good sign. The mistress of the house was going to make him wait, which probably meant she was going to see him. He took his pencil and the notes he had made at the meeting with Stancroft and his ladyfolk. Might as well use the time productively by reviewing what they'd discussed and marking any points that warranted further investigation.

He had been through all his notes and begun a list of next steps before the butler returned. "Lady Hardwicke will see you now," he said.

Ruadh put his notebook and pencil away. "Lead on," he told the butler.

The butler announced him in full form. "Major Douglas, Viscount Merrick, Master of Glencowan."

The lady who awaited him was a surprise. Lord Hardwicke had written to Mama that he had married his housekeeper. Ruadh had formed an image of an English version of the housekeeper in his father's house—on the far side of middle-aged, comfortably padded, cheerful, quietly competent, always ready with a bandage or snack for an adventurous boy.

Lady Hardwicke was a pretty brunette in, if Ruadh were to make a guess, her mid-thirties, much the same age as he was. She was attractively dressed in silk, her hair elaborately curled and pinned. Hard brown eyes examined Ruadh and warmed with feminine appreciation.

"You are Hector's grandson, Ruadh," she said, mangling the Scot's name as the English often did. Except for that, the hum in her low voice and something about her expression made it sound like an invitation to bed.

Ruadh ignored the tone and replied, "Yes, Lady Hardwicke, I am."

"You have been a persistent caller," she observed, her tone hardening as she realized she'd been rebuffed. "You have refused to accept my husband's disinterest in a visit from you."

"That is true, ma'am," Ruadh agreed. "My mother instructed me to see her father. She is understandably disturbed because he has ceased writing to her. You will sympathize, I am sure, with the feelings of a worried daughter. I am determined to see my grandfather and put my mother's concerns to rest."

Lady Hardwicke shook her head. "On your last visit, Lord Hardwicke tells me, you argued. My husband has been ill, Lord Merrick. I cannot have him upset. I refuse to allow you to visit."

"Then we are at an impasse, my lady, for I refuse to give up. I give you my word that I will not argue with my grandfather, no matter the provocation."

A flash of annoyance on the lady's face before she smoothed her expression again. "You must give this idea up, Lord Merrick. Tell your mother from me that her father has been ill but is now recovering and will undoubtedly write again when he is well. Better, give me your direction, and I shall write to her myself."

Ruadh inclined his head in partial acceptance. "Letters to my mother might be addressed to the Countess of Glencowan, Lannock Castle, Stranluce, Galloway. My mother's address has changed since her husband's elevation. But a letter to the address your husband has been using would be forwarded to the castle, my lady."

She was discomposed for a moment but recovered quickly. "Yes, of course." She stood. "If that is all, Lord Merrick?"

Ruadh stood too, and said, "No, my lady. I must insist on seeing my grandfather. If not today, then tomorrow."

"No, my lord. How clear do I need to be? I will not permit you to upset my husband."

Time to introduce another of Rose's suggestions. "I would be loath to air our family's disputes in public, Lady Hardwicke. However, if we cannot reach agreement without intervention, then I will need to involve a magistrate."

Again, her eyes betrayed her, with a flicker of alarm quickly suppressed. "With what complaint?" she scoffed. "That I have refused to allow the son of my husband's disowned daughter to disturb him in his sickbed?"

"That the Countess of Glencowan suspects malfeasance towards her father by his much younger wife," Ruadh improvised.

This time, the alarm he heard in her voice and saw in her eyes was accompanied by fear and then anger. "Get out," Lady Hardwicke hissed. "Get out before I have my footmen remove you."

"I will," Ruadh agreed, "to avoid damage to your furniture and your footmen. But I will return tomorrow at the same time as today, and if I am refused again, I will know you are attempting to hide something, and will return with the legal power to compel your compliance."

"Out!" Lady Hardwicke screeched. The butler opened the door and rushed into the room with such alacrity, that Ruadh was sure the man had been hovering there.

"My lady? Do you need help?"

"I was just leaving," Ruadh told him.

Another man pushed his way into the room—a young man with closely-cropped hair so white that at first glance Ruadh thought the man was bald. He glared at Ruadh from ice-blue eyes but spoke to the countess. "Do you want this man removed, my lady?"

Ruadh, out of habit, had already sized the young man up. Tall and strongly-built, he didn't move like a fighter. Still, he and the two footmen working together could probably remove Ruadh if they really tried. Almost without thinking about it, he changed his stance and tensed, ready for a fight.

"Lord Merrick was just leaving, Wolfendale," Lady Hardwicke said.

Wolfendale stepped out of Ruadh's way but scowled at him as he passed. Ruadh looked back into the room to see the man cross to Lady Hardwicke's side, the pair of them leaning slightly toward one another as they continued to glare in Ruadh's direction. The butler scurried around Ruadh to open the front door, and Ruadh tossed one last word at Lady Hardwicke. "Tomorrow," he said and left the house.

"I WISH YOU would stop introducing me as Lady Rosalind," said Rose to her brother Peter. "I am not entitled to the courtesy title."

"You are the daughter of an earl," Peter replied, mildly. "You and Viv are sisters. If she is Lady Vivienne and you are not Lady Rosalind, it draws attention to you."

"The earl was not married to my mother," Rose argued.

Viv intervened. "The earl was not my father," she pointed out, "and my mother was not married to the man who was."

"Yes, but your mother was married to my father when you were born," Rose insisted. "You have a legal right to be called by the courtesy title. I do not."

"You are both our sisters," Arial decreed. "The sins of your parents are not your fault and are the business of nobody outside the family. Rose, I know your stepmother made you feel as if you did not belong in the family, but you do, and we love you.

However, you need to realize that, if you insist on being called 'Miss Ransome', the questions raised affect us all, and particularly Vivienne."

"If you are worried about misleading suitors, Rose, it is an unnecessary concern," said Peter. "You have the Ransome bloodlines through our father, and anyone who wants an alliance with the Stancroft earldom through my sisters will have one if he marries either of you."

"I do not wish to marry anyone who cares about my blood lines or what my family can do for him," Rose objected.

"Then do not." Peter, who was the most indulgent of brothers, was impossible to shift once he had made up his mind. "But Rose, for Viv's sake, you will accept being called Lady Rosalind during your joint Seasons." That was clearly Peter's final word, and there was no point in continuing to argue.

Rose privately resolved, however, that any suitor—and she did not have one yet—would learn about her less-than-reputable origins before she agreed to marry him. She was annoyed that her mind went immediately to Lord Merrick when she thought of suitors. That he was the most fascinating man she had so far met in London was probably a reflection of the circumstances. He had saved her life—if he was, in fact, the Wolf. They had spent time discussing matters close to her heart, rather than the inanities that passed for conversation in polite circles.

Lord Merrick was not in London looking for a wife, and he was not interested in her, except as a source of information about herbalism, hospitals, and his grandfather. She needed to put him out of her mind. Perhaps tonight she might meet someone who preferred her rather ordinary looks to Viv's much more obvious beauty.

The sisters both had fair hair of a similar shade, but Viv's was just a touch more gold. Also, Viv's had a natural curl that was easily shaped into the ornate styles currently fashionable. Rose's hair hated pins and was prone to escape no matter how tightly it was confined. Viv's eyes were a blue that shaded into an unusual violet, whereas Ruth's were a rather ordinary blue, with nothing more to say about them.

Beyond that, Viv had the tall slender figure that was currently fashionable and that looked graceful in the current styles, whereas Rose was altogether more dumpy, with curves that, to her eyes at least, were out of proportion to her height.

Viv was also more sociable and outgoing. When gentlemen called or thronged around at a ball or a dinner, they were attracted by Viv's smile, her laugh, her amusing conversation. Rose had difficulty knowing what to say in response to a flirtatious sally, and preferred solitude or a quiet gathering with one or two close acquaintances as opposed to the large assemblies in which Viv flourished.

They were opposites in every way but had been the best of friends since they were babies, Rose being less than a year older than Viv, and the pair of them younger by more than a decade than Pauline, the next youngest child of the house.

Rose had managed to delay her own first Season for a year by claiming she wanted to wait and make her presentation with Viv. In truth, she would have happily done without a presentation or a Season altogether, but Peter had made that impossible by facing down a court official who raised the old rumors about her birth and Viv's, convincing him they were the work of a disappointed old besom with a poisonous tongue, and not to be regarded.

After that, Rose had had to go through with it for Viv's sake. Now, except for her work in the hospital, she was not enjoying the Season.

At least waiting for Viv meant she had her friend by her side for all the interminable social events that Arial and Pauline considered necessary. Putting up with being called 'Lady Rosalind' was not the first nor greatest compromise Rose had made for Viv.

Viv was excited about tonight's ball, and Rose allowed herself to be drawn into a discussion of which of their acquaintances might attend as they decided on the gowns to wear and the accessories. Ball preparation took up most of the rest of the evening, and it seemed no time at all before they were descending from their carriage and entering the house of Lord and Lady Snowden, the host and hostess of tonight's entertainment.

As close friends of Peter and Ariel, the Snowdens' party was warmly greeted. Margaret, Lady Snowden—also a countess in her own right—was a herbalist and Rose's mentor, but Rose could expect no cozy discussions about tisanes and tonics, pills, potions, and poultices, tonight. Margaret was very aware of what she owed to her position in Society. Tonight was about the ball and her guests.

The Stancroft party moved swiftly from the reception line into the ballroom. Peter and Ariel were their chaperones tonight, Pauline having asked to spend the night at home. They were soon besieged by gentlemen seeking a dance with Lady Vivienne. Enough of the losers also asked Rose for a dance that she did not need to fear sitting out all evening. Not that it would worry *her*. The best conversations were often those on the sidelines among those the fashionable thought of as the Season's rejects. But Peter *would* worry, and Viv would be upset.

Perhaps dancing would be more acceptable if there was someone special; someone with whom dancing was an element in the wider dance of courtship, as it was practiced among their class. But not only had Rose not caught the eye of potential suitors, no one had caught her eye.

Except for the Wolf and Ruadh Douglas, Viscount Merrick. The thought came unbidden, and she did her best to reject it. Was that why her senses kept telling her the two were the same man? Because she was attracted to them both?

Her attraction to the Wolf was an aberration. She had been frightened and in danger. He had saved her. Probably, if she saw him again, she would see that he was not nearly as tall and as broad as she had thought at the time.

As tall and as broad as Major Douglas, in fact. Lord Merrick, she meant. Still, he was not a suitor, and so, being attracted to him was pointless. He had not sought an introduction when they saw one another at the hospital. He had not called on her, but on her brother, and then only for the sake of his veterans. The son and heir of an earl had no place in his life for such as her.

When she saw him coming toward her through the crowds, she wondered if her thoughts had conjured him up, but it was the flesh and blood man, glorious in his full regimental uniform. The red of his kilt, the matching plaid he wore pinned to his shoulder and flowing down his back, and his checkered socks stood out against the background of the black and white worn by most of the other gentlemen. So did the gold frogging on his jacket, and the bright beacon of his hair.

More than one pair of female eyes tracked his progress across the floor.

RUADH HAD ASKED Lady Stancroft about their plans for the evening. He told himself that a social connection with the earl and his wife would be advantageous, but it was with the alluring sister that he imagined dancing. Indeed, with dancing in mind, he had asked his friend Nate, who had changed his bandages today, to add extra padding and bind his arm tightly so that bumping during vigorous exercise wasn't likely to bother the stitches.

And there she was, standing with the earl, his countess, and a girl who might be a friend, or perhaps another sister. *That girl doesn't look like my Rose.* He caught the mental slip. Not his Rose. He didn't mean it in the sense of a deep connection. After all, he scarcely knew the lady. Lady Rosalind, he should have said.

His internal argument left him off-balance as he reached the family group, greeting Lady Stancroft first, then her lord, and lastly Lady Rosalind.

"Vivienne, may I present Lord Merrick, the Master of Glencowan?" said Stancroft. "Douglas, another of my sisters, Lady

Vivienne Ransome. My sister Pauline Turner is not here this evening."

Lady Vivienne was a pretty girl in an ordinary sort of way. The sort of girl he'd seen at every fashionable event in London to which he'd been inveigled by friends. Fair curls, pale skin, and a figure like a stick with only the smallest of bumps to indicate she was female. He bowed politely. "I am delighted to meet you, Lady Vivienne. Lord Stancroft must be the envy of the gentlemen here to be the escort of three such lovely ladies."

Lady Stancroft wore yet another mask, this one ornamented with jewels that complemented those she wore at her wrist, her ears, and on her neck. Did she always wear the mask? He wondered how badly she was scarred.

But even as he answered Stancroft's question about his reception at his grandfather's house, his eyes kept sliding back to Lady Rosalind who was, in his opinion, the finest jewel in Stancroft's collection. "I shall return tomorrow, and we shall see what happens," he finished explaining.

Should he ask Lady Rosalind for a dance? He was certain she must have already given all of them away, and indeed, a man had just asked Lady Vivienne and been turned away with a charming disclaimer that she had no dances left.

When the man walked away without speaking to Lady Rosalind, his assumption was confirmed. Then the orchestra began to play, another man whisked Lady Vivienne off to the dance floor, and Lady Rosalind remained, chatting quietly with her sister-in-law.

"Lady Rosalind," Ruadh said, hurriedly, before he could talk himself out of it, "would you honor me with this dance?" Now she would tell him that she did not dance tonight or some such claptrap.

But she didn't. She smiled and said, "I would like that, Major Douglas."

It was a quadrille, a dance performed by four couples, and they quickly found a group of three pairs lacking a fourth. She danced with grace and enthusiasm, her bountiful breasts performing an interesting jig of their own that made him grateful to be in a kilt so that his body's response was concealed.

He mostly managed to keep his eyes on hers, rather than letting them slip below her neck and was rewarded by her lovely eyes, which in the light of the candles danced with golden flames as she smiled at him.

The dance was vigorous, so they were unable to talk. The arm protested some of the movements, but not enough to inhibit him. As he walked the lady back to her brother's side, he had just enough time to beg her for the supper dance. He was surprised when it was available. What was wrong with the gentlemen of London? He couldn't understand why her every dance was not taken, as her sister said hers was.

Some remnants of his mother's teaching remained with him enough that he did his duty by other young ladies while waiting for his next dance with Lady Rosalind. To come to the ball and dance with only one lady was to call attention to her, and to raise expectations with her, her family, and the onlookers.

The idea didn't panic him. He poked at it as if it was a tooth that had once been sore, waiting for the wince and the recoil. Was he seriously considering Lady Rosalind as a possible wife? *No.* Of course not. He was too old and too broken. He didn't know her well enough. She was too young for him—not young enough to be his daughter, but still much younger. Furthermore, she was English, and close to her family, but his wife would have to live in Galloway.

He was only here for a dance or two. That was all there could be.

VIV INSISTED THAT those who sought her favor must treat Rose with respect. Indeed, she had frozen one gentleman from her court when he asked Rose for a dance and spent it leering at her breasts and had dismissed another who had made an insulting reference to Rose's irregular parentage.

Peter might think Rose's parentage was a secret, but it had only been a few years since Pauline's mother, their father's second wife, had attacked Peter by making Rose's base-born status the talk of the ton. Some of the men courting Viv were old enough to remember, and those who were not on the Town back then had relatives who were.

Still, Viv's followers got the hint, and the cleverest of them did their best to charm Rose, so she would speak well of them to her sister.

That, surely, was Lord Merrick's scheme. She gave him credit for his tact. Not once during the supper waltz did he mention Viv or stare at Rose's breasts, so Rose felt he deserved a reward when they went into supper. She suggested they join the table where Viv was already seated with one of her admirers, Lord Clough. Lord Clough was heir to an earl, and currently front runner in the pack vying for Viv's attention.

He looked up as Rose and Lord Merrick arrived at the table, lifting a quizzing glass to stare at Lord Merrick. "Begad!" he declared. "Are the Scots invading?"

Lord Merrick, bless him, was amused. "Of course. It is our turn."

The implication that the Scots had been invaded by the English went right over Lord Clough's head. He was still frowning when Viv made the introductions. "Viscount Merrick, meet Viscount Clough. Lord Merrick is a major with the 175th Scots Foot, Lord Clough, and is in London studying hospitals for injured veterans. Lord Clough is a notable whip, Lord Merrick, and a member of the Four Horse Club."

It was a good effort on Viv's part, but what a mismatched pair! Lord Clough must have noticed that the two descriptions made him sound like a fribble next to the major, for his lip curled and he commented, "A highland regiment, I take it since you are wearing a skirt."

Viv pressed her lips together and glared at Lord Clough. "Sir, if you would prefer not to sit with my sister and her escort, I give you leave to go."

Good for Viv. Of course, the young viscount realized he had put his foot in his mouth and stumbled through an apology, first to Viv and then, at her prompting, to Rose and Lord Merrick. By this time Lord Merrick had pulled out a chair for Rose and seen her seated. He returned a clever answer to Lord Clough's seemingly sincere, "I beg your pardon, Merrick. I spoke out of turn."

"You did, Lord Clough, but I can see why." He cast an amused glance towards Viv, and then said to Lord Clough, "Let us make common cause in service to the ladies. Ladies, shall Clough and I bring you a selection of whatever we can find at the buffet?"

Rose and Viv agreed, and the two men strolled off. "What do you think of Lord Merrick?" Rose asked her sister.

"He is nice, I suppose," Viv conceded. "I like that he did not let Lord Clough make him angry. I suppose, though, it would not do for a soldier of his rank to be too easily annoyed. And he is old, of course. A young man would lose his temper more easily."

"He is not old," Rose protested.

"He is much older than us," Viv pointed out.

"Not more than fifteen years," Rose said. She had looked him up in Arial's copy of Debrett's. He wasn't there, but his father was recorded as the second son of the 5th Earl of Glencowan, together with the date of his marriage, which was in seventeen ninety-two, so even if Lord Merrick had been born just nine months after the wedding, he could not be more than thirty-four years of age now.

"Fifteen years!" Viv commented, with a shudder. "Too old for me. Mind you, it is not me he is interested in."

Rose said no more, certain that Viv was wrong and that she would change her mind once Lord Merrick turned those compelling eyes on her, but when he and Lord Clough returned with four glasses of champagne, and a willing footman carrying a tray of full plates, he continued to pay most of his attention to her and not her sister.

He and Lord Clough must have reached an understanding while negotiating the buffet, for the younger man's hostility was gone, and he even asked a couple of questions about the uniform that Lord Merrick wore.

The pattern of the cloth that made up both the major's kilt and the fall of color from his shoulder was the regimental tartan, Lord Merrick explained. As for the silver brooch in the form of a wolf's head that pinned the plaid in place on his shoulder, he said, "It is the Glencowan wolf. My grandfather gave it to me when I went to war. Oddly enough, it is traditionally worn by the Master of Glencowan."

"What does that mean," Viv asked. "Master of Glencowan?"

"In Scotland, my lady," Lord Merrick replied, "the heir to a title is called Master of whatever the title is. My father is now Earl of Glencowan, so I am Master of Glencowan."

"I could happily adopt that tradition," Lord Clough said cheerfully. "Master of Rule has a ring to it."

At that point, Lord Merrick noticed that Rose had finished her champagne. He offered her another, but she asked for a lemonade, and he went off to find it. He was not gone for long, but in that time, Viv and Lord Clough had moved on to discussing a garden party they had all been to the previous weekend.

Rose, as usual when it came to social events, had little to say. Lord Merrick returned with four glasses. "I did not ask your preference, Lady Vivienne, or yours, Clough, but the drinks are here if you want them. Lady Rosalind?" He passed her one of the tall cool glasses, in which the cloudy lemonade had been served over chunks of ice.

After thanking him for the lemonade, which Viv accepted but Lord Clough ignored, the other two picked up their previous conversation. Rose thought it a little rude, because Lord Merrick had not been present and probably knew none of the people mentioned.

Lord Merrick showed no sign of annoyance. Indeed, he turned to Rose with every evidence of pleasure. "How did you become interested in herb craft, my lady?"

Rose gave a brief answer which led to another question, and before she realized, she was telling him all about how their hostess, Lady Snowden, had learned her craft from her mother, who had treated Ariel during her long convalescence after she was horribly burned in a house fire.

"Pauline learned about growing herbs from Lady Snowden," Rose explained. "She is more interested in her work with roses, though, whereas I was fascinated by what herbs could do for us in the still room and the kitchen. So, I pestered Lady Snowden until she taught me, and when I am in London, I go with her on her rounds."

Viv broke into their conversation at that point. "Lady Snowden was delighted to have you as a pupil, Rose, as you well know. She is very proud of you, as am I. I am nothing but a butterfly, Lord Merrick, decorative but not good for much else. My sister is not only pretty, but useful as well."

"Viv!" Rose protested. "You are far more than that." At the same time, Lord Clough exclaimed that he liked butterflies. Rose caught the look her sister sent her and held her tongue. Viv, for some reason, enjoyed having her courtiers underestimate her.

"Many butterflies are very decorative," Lord Merrick acknowledged, "but a man looking for a bride, a mother to his children, and a life companion wants more substance than that. Unless he is a gommy."

Rose was intrigued. "What is a gommy?"

"A fool. An idiot," Lord Merrick explained. He glanced around the busy supper room. "I've known a few."

He noticed Rose's plate was empty and offered her the still half-full platter.

"No, thank you, my lord. I have had sufficient, and if I eat any more, I shall be unable to enjoy the rest of the evening."

"I would like to ask you to dance again, Lady Rosalind," he confided, "but I am told it would break a rule and set in train the destruction of the entire social order."

His hyperbole, delivered in a mournful tone, set Rose giggling. Now he would ask her to persuade Viv to dance with him, but he would not succeed, for she had given all her dances elsewhere, this evening. Still, he had been so attentive and such good company, that she would ask Viv to be kind to him on the next occasion. Even if it did give Rose a pang.

"Rose, are you ready?" said Viv. "The dancing is about to start again, and Lord Clough is going to escort me back to Arial so my partners can find me. And you, if you are coming with me."

"May I have the privilege of escorting you, my lady?" Lord Merrick asked.

Rose waited for Viv to reject him and then realized he was looking at her. Her heart fluttered. "Yes. Yes, thank you."

As she walked with her hand on his arm, he leaned towards her, bringing his mouth closer to her ear so that she could hear him over the tuning of instruments and the buzz of conversation. *Here it came. The request to intercede with Viv on his behalf.*

"Lady Rosalind," he said, "I very much enjoyed our waltz. Would it be presumptuous to ask what entertainment you are attending tomorrow night? And if there is dancing, may I beg a waltz?"

Chapter Four

As Ruadh passed the Stancroft townhouse on his way to see his grandfather, he remembered Lady Rosalind's reaction to his request for a waltz. He had been thinking about it ever since the night before—that, and about how easy it was to talk to her. She had been relaxed in his company, he'd thought, but then he asked his question. She had been at first surprised and then appeared worried.

She had given him the information he asked for... they were going to the theatre tonight but would be at the Dellborough Ball the following night, and yes, she would grant him another quadrille and another waltz, and one would be the supper dance.

He should be delighted, but he had spent much of his wakeful night wondering why his invitation bothered her. Indeed, thoughts of Lady Rosalind had distracted him throughout his patrol of the rookeries streets he thought of as his own to protect. It was just as well the night had been quiet, and the few malefactors out and about had fled at the first sight of the Wolf.

Which was all to the good. Quite apart from his mind not being focused, his arm had been troubling him more than he expected. And there had been people out on his patch hunting him. The boy he had saved two nights earlier had warned him some bounty hunters had been asking questions and were out in the night waiting for something to happen. "I didn't tell them nothin', Wolf. Ain't nobody sayin' nothin'. But watch out."

For now, he had to push all that to the back of his mind, for here was his grandfather's door. He plied the knocker and waited.

The butler opened the door and let him immediately. "Lady Hardwicke is expecting you, Lord Merrick. This way, if you please."

Instead of leading Ruadh to the drawing room where he had met with Lady Hardwicke last time, the butler continued straight on up the stairs to the second floor, and into a wide passage, gloomy and shadowed because the only light came from the stairwell behind him. A female figure was waiting near a door at the end of the passage.

The passage struck him as bare. He thought he detected slightly lighter squares of wallpaper where he might have expected paintings. There were no candles in the sconces and only a few items of furniture. Odd. He wondered what he would find if he opened some of the doors he passed.

"Good afternoon, Lady Hardwicke," he greeted his grandfather's wife.

"Good day, Lord Merrick." Today, her voice was all business. "You will remember, please, that you are entering a sick room. You must not raise your voice, and you will not be permitted to remain for long."

Ruadh bowed an acknowledgment, which she must have taken as agreement, for she opened the door beside her, and led the way inside.

The room was even dimmer than the passage. Lady Hardwicke picked up a holder with a single candle from a table by the door. By its inadequate light, Ruadh could just make out a huddled figure in the old-fashioned four-poster bed, propped up on pillows and covered with blankets. The bed curtains were closed on the other side of the bed and beyond them, heavy drapes covered most of one wall—presumably covering windows.

"Your grandson has come to visit, my love," Lady Hardwicke cooed. "Step over here, Lord Merrick." She put a hand up to shade the flame of the candle, casting the figure on the bed into deeper shadow. "My husband cannot bear bright light," she told Ruadh in a hushed voice. She stepped away to place the candle somewhere it was masked by the bed curtains.

From his position next to the bed, all Ruadh could see in the dark cavern of the bed were the dim rectangles of the pillows and the darker shape of a head against them.

"My lord," he said, formally, "I was sorry to hear you have been ill. I trust you are recovering?"

"Slowly, Ruadh," said his grandfather, the voice low and husky. "Merrick, I should say. My Anna-Louise is a countess now, my wife tells me. Congratulations, Merrick."

Ruadh swallowed a surge of distaste. *Congratulations on the death of my uncle and my cousins?* He should not take offense. The man's reaction was not unusual. "My mother asked me to call, sir," he said. "She was concerned when her last two letters were not answered. She will be sorry to hear the reason." *She still loves you, you old curmudgeon.*

"Thank her for me," said the earl. "I hope to be able to write again soon. My eyes, you know. Can't stand the light. Perhaps I will dictate a letter to Yvonne, my wife, and she can write it for me."

"I am sure my mother will be pleased, sir."

The countess interrupted. "That is enough, my love. You tire so easily. Lord Merrick?"

"I am glad to see you, sir," Ruadh said, bowing. "Farewell. I hope you shall be much recovered when I next call."

Ruadh's eyes had adjusted enough that he could easily see his way back to the door, though the countess left her candle behind as she followed him. She stopped at the door to say to her husband, "I shall return shortly, my love."

He waited for her outside the bedchamber, and when she had closed the door, he asked, "What do the physicians say about my grandfather's chances of recovery, Lady Hardwicke?"

"They believe he will never again be as vigorous, Lord Merrick, but that he will improve over time. We hope that his eyes will grow more tolerant to light and that he will sleep less often and spend more time out of bed."

She dabbed at her eyes with a cloth. "It is hard to see him laid so low. It is why I am so protective of him. I apologize if I was harsh with you yesterday, Lord Merrick."

"It was not my intention to upset you or my grandfather," Ruadh told her. Perhaps he owed her an apology, too, but he rather thought not. Perhaps, if he had not heard what Rose had said about the earl, he would have accepted the scene that had just been performed for his benefit, but again, he rather thought not. He would need to retreat to decide on his next moves.

She began walking, and he kept up with her.

"May I call again, my lady? Perhaps at this time tomorrow?"

"The day after that, I think, Lord Merrick." She frowned. "I do not wish to be inhospitable, but my husband's wellbeing must come first. I trust you have friends or other family with whom you can stay?" He wished he could see her eyes. It was hard to judge whether this was an interrogation with purpose or casual conversation. Did she want to know if he had people who would miss him? Or how to find him at his most defenseless? Or was he being over-suspicious?

He had one way to find out where she would go with the conversation if she thought he was friendless. "Not here in London, my lady," Ruadh admitted, "but I have rented rooms, and I shall not be here long."

"You came to London to see my husband?" she asked

"No, ma'am. I had some business to complete here before I resigned my commission." Not untrue. He would continue being polite until he had enough information to take action if it was truly necessary.

"I trust your business is going well?" she asked.

"I expect to have it all settled within a week. I'll be on my way north after that. Without friends or family in London, I have nothing to keep me here once my business is over, but I should like to take my mother good news of her father." There. If she had malignant intent, that should be enough to tempt her.

They had come downstairs while talking and were now in the entry hall. The butler emerged from somewhere to hand Ruadh his hat and coat. He wished Lady Hardwicke a good day and allowed himself to be ushered into the street.

On the off chance the lady might send someone to watch him out of sight, he continued past the Stanhope front steps, along the row, and around the corner. Then he hurried back along the lane between the back gardens and the mews, counting until he got to the Stancroft townhouse.

He was not going to miss a chance to see Lady Rosalind, and perhaps she could help him make sense of the inconsistencies between what she had said about Lord Hardwicke, and what Ruadh had observed.

The Stancrofts had made the most of their long, narrow garden. Ruadh passed a thriving vegetable garden, a row of fruit trees, a berry cage, and a substantial glasshouse before coming out from between two large shrubs onto a path that led between flower beds to the house.

A large shade tree hid him from anyone looking out of the Hardwicke windows and also obscured the part of the Stancroft terrace closest to that neighbor. He continued towards the house, accompanied by the perfumes of more flowers than he could name, though some of them, at least, were roses.

Once beyond the tree, he was brought up short by an unexpected sight. Not Lady Rosalind, leaning close to the trellis between her terrace and the next. He was pleased to see the lady—if he'd still had a heart, he'd have described the odd feeling in his chest as his heart bounding—but what stopped him in his tracks was the man she was talking to.

Imperfectly seen through the trellis was a man in an invalid chair. Bent and shrunken though the man was, Ruadh recognized his grandfather.

⁕

LORD HARDWICKE SAW Lord Merrick first. "Ruaa!" he said, his eyes fixed down the garden. "Ruaa!"

Rose looked over her shoulder and there he was. Lord Merrick, leaving the path to cross the lawn to the wall between Peter's townhouse and that of the Hardwickes, then hurrying toward her in the shelter of the wall.

In moments, he had joined her on the terrace. "Lady Rosalind," he greeted her, and bowed briefly over her hand, his eyes fixed on the elderly invalid next door.

She stepped to one side and waved him toward the trellis. "He is glad to see you," she said unnecessarily, for Lord Hardwick had a grin spread across the side of his face that still worked and was bobbing his head up and down and flapping the hand he could still use.

"Ruaa!" he repeated.

Lord Merrick dropped to one knee to bring his head level with that of the old man. "Grandfather, I bring greetings and best wishes from my mother. She is concerned about you."

"Goo' gir'," Lord Hardwicke said. "Shorry. Dell 'er shorry."

Lord Merrick slid his eyes sideways and up, to catch Rose's eye, a plea for help in his own. "Good girl, he said," she explained. "Sorry. Tell her sorry."

"You are sorry for how you treated my mother?" Lord Merrick asked, his voice stern.

Lord Hardwicke nodded, and tears welled in his eyes, some of them spilling down his cheeks. Lord Merrick softened. "She has forgiven you, Grandfather," he said.

"Goo' gir'," Lord Hardwicke repeated.

"Better than any of us deserve," Lord Merrick agreed. "She will be sorry to hear that you are so unwell."

"Dying," Lord Hardwicke corrected him. "Abou' dime. Ruaa, shdop Efong." He waved his good hand towards the house. "Aw' yours. No' for 'er. No' Wolf."

Both men turned their eyes to Rose.

"Lord Hardwicke says that he is dying, and it is about time. Then he wants you to stop someone. Efong?"

"Yvonne?" Lord Merrick asked his grandfather, who nodded. "Lady Hardwicke's name is Yvonne," Lord Merrick told Rose.

That made sense. "Lord Hardwicke says the house is all yours."

Lord Hardwicke objected to that with a grunt and a head shake.

Rose made a guess. "All that he has is yours?" Yes, that fetched a nod. "All yours. Not for her. Not Wolf's. I think he means his valet, whose name is Wolfendale."

The old man nodded his agreement. "Efong and Wolf. Shdop dem."

"I will stop them," Lord Merrick agreed, without waiting for Rose to translate. "I will find out what they are up to, and I will get you away from them."

"Be carefu'," warned the invalid. "Dangerous."

From his skeptical look, Lord Merrick did not think he had much to fear from a woman and a valet. Rose hoped he was not being overconfident.

"Proud of you, Ruaa," Lord Hardwicke said.

At that moment, they were interrupted as a pair of footmen came out onto the terrace. "It's back inside for you, old man," said one, as he took the handles on the invalid chair and turned it towards the house.

Lord Merrick had ducked out of sight behind a large pot. Rose was still in plain view and flushed as the footmen sneered at her. "Mind your own business, your ladyship," said one. Perhaps the ironic twist she heard in the honorific was in her imagination, but she did not think so.

The man with her heard it too, for he made as if to stand. Rose put a hand out, signaling caution. He must have agreed, for he subsided.

"'uv you. 'Uv Anga-Leez," Lord Hardwicke shouted.

"Shut up, old man. No one can understand you. Nobody cares," mocked the footman who was lifting the front of the invalid chair into the house. The other footman lifted the back wheels over the threshold and closed the door behind them.

The footman was wrong. Lord Merrick cared. And Rose understood most of what Lord Hardwicke said. *Love you.* That was easy. But who else did he love?

"Anna-Louise." Lord Merrick had straightened to his full height. His shoulders were rigid and his jaw set. The gaze he sent after the footmen left no doubt about his anger, but his voice was mild as he said, "My mother's name. He wants me to tell her that he loves her. Lady Rosalind, how long has my grandfather been outside?"

"He was here when I came out to check my seedlings," Lady Rosalind said. "That must have been an hour ago, so at least an hour."

"May we go inside, my lady?" Lord Merrick asked. "I need to talk about what I found when I visited next door, and I would welcome your thoughts, and those of your brother and his wife."

"REUBEN, WHERE IS my brother?" Lady Rosalind asked the footman who was polishing the brass finials on the stair posts.

Ruadh nearly greeted the man but remembered in time that the young footman had no idea they had met. "He is in the drawing room with her ladyship, my lady," said Reuben.

"Order tea, please, Reuben. Or would you prefer coffee or a wine, Lord Merrick? Or something else?"

"Tea would be pleasant, thank you," Ruadh told her.

She nodded and led Ruadh up two flights of steps to the next floor. The drawing room door was open, and Ruadh followed her into the room, where Stancroft was reading the newspaper, and Stancroft's other three ladies were busy with activities of their own. Lady Stancroft was using a lap desk, her pen moving busily over a sheet of paper. Lady Vivienne was cutting out paper—making silhouettes, Ruadh would guess. And Miss Turner was reading a letter or some similar document.

"Sisters, Peter, I have brought Lord Merrick to see you all. He has a problem he hopes we can help him with," Lady Rosalind said. "I believe everyone has met him except Pauline. Pauline, may I present Lord Merrick? Sir, my sister, Miss Pauline Turner."

He had met her on a dark London street, but she, of course, did not know that. He gave the expected shallow bow. "I apologize for interrupting your afternoon."

"Not at all, Lord Merrick," said Lady Stancroft. "Rose, will you ring the bell for refreshments? Lord Merrick, please be seated."

"I have ordered tea," Rose told the countess.

"I did not hear the door knocker," Stancroft observed.

"I came up the path from the mews lane," Ruadh confessed. "I was next door visiting my grandfather, and I suspected that Lady Hardwicke might set her servants to watching where I went, so I avoided your front door, and thus learned I had not been visiting my grandfather at all."

Stancroft's eyes opened wider at that. "This is the problem to which Rose referred? Your grandfather?"

"We have been concerned," Lady Stancroft commented. "Rose and Pauline have become well-acquainted with Lord Hardwicke through their joint interest in the gardens, and have tried to visit several times since we heard he had suffered an apoplexy."

"We were turned away," Miss Turner said. "We have, however, been able to see him since the servants have begun putting him outside on a fine day."

"He has been distressed about Lady Hardwicke," Rose said. "Exactly what worries him is unclear. His speech is hard to understand, though he is improving."

A knock on the door interrupted Stancroft as he was about to speak. As servants streamed in with tea makings and plates of little sweet and savory treats, he said, "Your regiment has been serving in Ireland, I believe."

Of all the topics he might have introduced for conversation in front of the servants, that was close to the top of the list of matters Ruadh would rather avoid. "I have been in Ireland with my regiment for close to ten years," he said.

Perhaps Stancroft picked up something from Ruadh's tone, for he commented, "A difficult service. You are currently on leave?"

Another difficult topic. "I have been. Since my father's elevation, my parents have asked me to resign my commission and return home." To his ears, that sounded calm enough, but perhaps not, for Stancroft grimaced.

"A good plan to learn the estate while you are still the heir."

But it turned out, Stancroft was speaking of his own experience. "I served in the Peninsula and at Waterloo and came home when my father died." For a moment his gaze was far away, and Lady Stancroft paused in her tea-making to put a gentle hand on his. He turned his hand over and met her sweet smile with his own.

The heart Ruadh was sure he didn't have ached in his chest at the intimate connection they showed in that one moment. What would it be like to have someone who cared? Someone who knew when his mind wandered back to battlefields and misery, and was there to draw him home again with a touch?

The servants had withdrawn again by this time. Rose returned to their previous conversation with a question. "You have concerns about your grandfather, Lord Merrick? May I ask what you have learned?"

"Lady Hardwicke led me upstairs to a darkened passage and a darker bedchamber," He explained to the group. "She said the apoplexy had left Grandfather with weak eyes, so even a little light hurt him. His words to me were quite clear and I remembered that Lady Rosalind had implied he could not speak. As we talked, Lady Hardwicke was keen to know when I planned to leave London, and whether I have friends here."

Stancroft's frown had deepened. "For what purpose did they deceive you?"

"That is the question," Ruadh agreed. "I can only think that Grandfather had something to say to me they did not want me to hear."

"His speech has improved," Rose said. "Today, he warned Lord Merrick about his wife and his valet."

Ruadh nodded. "He asked me to stop them, and told me to be careful."

"I think, my dear," Stancroft said to his wife, "we must share the servants' gossip about Lady Hardwicke and Wolfenden, the valet."

"An affair?" Ruadh asked. That was the most obvious conclusion, confirmed by his own observation of the pair leaning together as he left them a couple of days ago.

"Gossip would have it so," Lady Stancroft said, her expression showing she was uncomfortable with the topic.

"Lady Hardwicke told Lord Hardwicke that Phillip said it would be a mercy to put a pillow over Lord Hardwicke's face." Lady Rosalind's cheeks colored as she admitted, "They were on their terrace, and I overheard because I was behind the pots. Phillip is the name of the valet."

"That would be simple," Stancroft mused. "Why haven't they done it? Squeamish about taking a life?" He looked around at his audience. "Sorry. I did not mean to offend your sensibilities."

"Nonsense." It was the third sister, Lady Vivienne, who had not so far contributed to the conversation. "If you start treating us like ninnies, Peter, *then* we shall be offended. It is a good question. One would think Lady Hardwicke would enjoy being a rich widow."

"That is what she said," Lady Rosalind commented. "'I wish

you had died in your fit. Then I would be a rich widow.' But when we met him in the garden, Lord Hardwick said she was not in his will, and he told Lord Merrick he wanted him to inherit everything."

"I wondered if they are selling the paintings from the wall," Ruadh said. "The walls have patches of a different shade, as if paintings have been removed. There were also fewer furnishings than one would expect, though that might be a matter of taste."

"Does your grandfather have children other than your mother, my lord?" asked Lady Stancroft.

"My mother was an only child," Ruadh replied. "I never thought to ask Lady Hardwicke... have they been married for long?"

Lady Stancroft frowned as she considered the question. "A little over a year, perhaps?"

Lady Vivienne spoke up again. "They were not married when we were in Town the year before last, but they were by the time we came up last Spring. Lord Merrick, you probably know that Lady Hardwicke was the housekeeper next door before your grandfather married her."

Ruadh nodded.

"She was always so nice to him," Lady Rosalind commented. "Right up until he was helpless."

"If she has a child," said Lady Vivienne, "the child will probably inherit. The title and entailed properties, at least. Perhaps everything, depending on his lordship's will. That might be why they cannot kill him. Yet."

"Surely not," Arial protested. "That sounds like a plot from one of your gothic novels, Viv."

"No more gothic than we have lived through," Lady Vivienne retorted. Ruadh was considering the suggestion and deciding it made sense but put Lady Vivienne's remark away to think about later.

"Whatever the reason, Merrick needs to get his grandfather out from under Lady Hardwicke's control," Stancroft said.

"Merrick, I have a suggestion. There's a husband-and-wife team of inquiry agents I've used before. Very good. Very discreet. You need evidence to put Lady Hardwicke and the valet out of the house and replace them with people you can trust. Perhaps some of the other servants, too. The Wakefields can find you that evidence."

That was the second time someone had mentioned the Wakefields to him. The third, if he counted the boy who told him people were hunting for him, though that might have been a coincidence. Still, nobody except Nate knew that Ruadh was the Wolf, and Nate would never betray him. Perhaps it was time to retire the Wolf, as he would have to do soon enough anyway.

As to his grandfather, if Nate and Stancroft both agreed that the inquiry agents were effective and trustworthy, that was good enough for him.

"If you are able to give me their direction, Stancroft, I should like to engage them."

Chapter Five

"MERRICK DANCED WITH you again last night," Peter observed at breakfast. "Twice, and one of them the supper dance."

"Yes," Rose said. "He asked me at the ball a few days ago. And last night he asked if he might take me driving this after-noon."

"Did he, indeed?" asked Peter. "Is he courting you, Rose?"

Rose pondered that. He had certainly been attentive. He had not danced with Vivienne at all, and he had not danced with anyone twice. Indeed, he seemed to go out of his way to pick ladies who were not usually invited to dance. Debutantes who were young, shy, and spotty. Companions long past their last prayers and sinking into oblivion. Several wives faithful to their husbands but fond of dancing.

It had crossed Rose's mind to wonder whether she was an-other of his charity cases, but she was beginning to hope that was not the case. No one else had been begged for four dances between the two balls. No one else was asked for a waltz, or for the privilege of escorting her into supper. He had directed the smoldering heat in his eyes in her direction and in her direction only. And now he had asked her to come for a drive.

She had not allowed herself to think as far ahead as courtship, however. "Usually, the men who pay me attention are trying to curry favor with Viv," she told Peter.

"Lord Merrick has no interest in me," Viv said.

"Lord Merrick has eyes for no one except Rose," Arial observed.

"The question is," said Peter, "how does Rose feel about Lord Merrick?"

Rose could feel her cheeks heating. "The question is a little beforehand, is it not? Lord Merrick has not asked to court me."

Arial gave a quick shake of her head. "I disagree, Rose. If you think you might be developing an affection for Lord Merrick, then yes, wait and see what happens. If you are sure he is not someone you could tie yourself to for the rest of your life, now is the time to gently discourage him."

"He's rather old," Viv observed.

"Thank you," Peter said, dryly. He, Rose knew, would be thirty-seven years of age on his next birthday.

Viv refused to be squelched. "You are twice as old as I am, Peter, and Rose is only a year older than me."

"It is a sizeable age gap," Arial agreed, "but Rose is mature for her age."

It is rather annoying to be talked about instead of to. "I am here, you know," she pointed out.

Arial turned the tables on her rather neatly. "Do you mind the age gap, Rose? Would you like Lord Merrick to court you?"

She thought about the question and the man. Ruadh, as she had been calling him in her own mind since she first heard of him from his grandfather. Ruadh, who was as much of a hero as his grandfather believed. Ruadh, with his haunted eyes, with his warrior's face and figure, that looked as if all excess flesh had worn away, leaving only muscle and skin stretched over the bone. With the innate kindness that led him to offer dances to the overlooked and to agonize over the plight of an old man who he had no reason to like.

"I do not see why he would," she said. "What do I have to

offer a man like him? As Viv says, he is a man grown, in the prime of his life. He has traveled the world and has had experiences I cannot imagine. Even if he finds me attractive…" She thought about the heat she had seen in his eyes and had to acknowledge, if only to herself, that he was attracted to her. "It does not mean he plans to act on his attraction."

"He had better not," Peter growled. "Not unless he has offered for you. Not unless you have his ring on your finger."

"What do *you* want?" Arial asked, with gentle insistence.

I want Ruadh, Rose realized. "I would like to go driving with Lord Merrick and see what happens after that. He has said he intends to return to Scotland, soon. If he does, then at least I will have had an enjoyable drive and a pleasant partner for several dances."

If he did not intend anything more than a flirtation to while away his time in London, he would leave Rose with a bruised heart, but so be it. She would not discourage him now and precipitate the loss she fully expected to suffer but would build a few memories to keep her company in the coming years. One waltz, one conversation, one drive at a time. Perhaps, if she was very fortunate, one kiss?

RUADH DIDN'T KNOW what had got into him. He had been talking to Rose—to Lady Rosalind—about the activities of the Season and heard himself asking if he could take her for a drive. It was as if his much younger and more hopeful self had taken over his voice.

He managed to borrow a curricle and pair from an intrigued and curious Nate, and on the way to the Stancrofts' to pick the lady up, he berated himself for raising expectations. But how bad could it be?

In a few days, maybe a week at most, he would leave for

Scotland, the problem of his grandfather solved. In the meantime, he could fill his mind and his senses with the lovely Rose—sights, scents, and sounds to take out and examine in the lonely years ahead.

She did not keep him waiting when he pulled up, appearing almost immediately wearing a smart blue walking dress and matching bonnet, with a parasol in a lighter blue. Her promptness was just as well, for Nate's team was high-bred and frisky, and he did not want to leave them.

Ruadh needed to give them most of his attention during the drive to the park, for they objected to the slow pace that was appropriate in the heavy traffic, took offense at any horse that passed them, even going in the other direction, and were inclined to panic when a fluttering scarf escaped a peddler's tray and blew across the road in front of them.

Once in the park, Ruadh said, "If you have no objection, my lady, I'd like to take one of the less-traveled carriageways, and let these young lads trot off a few of their fidgets."

"Yes, they will appreciate that," Rose agreed. "They are too excited to remember their manners, at the moment."

He smiled as he turned the curricle onto a side path that wound between trees and released the reins to give them their heads and step up their pace. Rose lifted her face to the air. Her own smile was not directed at him. She seemed to be smiling at the pleasure of the air rushing past her, the horses suddenly pulling in harmony under the firm control of the driver, the trees passing quickly, but not so fast that the pair of them could not admire their beauty.

That was certainly what Ruadh was enjoying. That, and being with Lady Rose, whose quiet beauty he had missed noticing at first, but who was more and more appealing to all his senses, and to his imagination, as he came to know her better.

The pathway they were on came to an end with a sweeping circle around a summerhouse. "Would you like to walk for a time, Lady Rosalind?" Ruadh asked, the words leaving him even as the impulse entered his brain. "I saw a little pond off to the right that might be interesting."

"That would be delightful," she agreed.

So Ruadh told Nate's groom who was standing on a little platform behind the curricle, to trot the horses back and forth several times, the length of the path, until they were ready to behave themselves once it was time to negotiate the traffic again. A footpath wound into the trees near the summer house. With Lady Rose's hand on his arm, he headed along the footpath in the direction of the pond.

He was already regretting his impulsive decision. Yet another impulsive decision in a string of them, and all of them involving his pretty Rose. *No! Not mine. It would not be fair to the lady.*

"I hope this will take us where we want to go, my lady," he said.

"We cannot get lost, Lord Merrick. If the worst comes to the worst, we need only to retrace our steps."

True enough, but the danger lay in getting lost, not in the park but in the beautiful woman on his arm. Her innocent touch was the lure into a thicket of indecision. He had thought his mind made up. This lovely girl deserved marriage or nothing, and Ruadh was not fit to marry.

Though being the heir to Glencowan meant he would have to take a wife. Broken or not, it was his job to hold the earldom in his turn, and to father the next heir. While his head protested that he could not burden a lady he liked by making her his wife, his heart was already coming up with reasons why Lady Rose was the only possible contender for the position.

"Look," she said, as they turned a corner. "Water."

"And ducks," he commented. They had found the pond, and a few more steps brought them into a clearing where three paths converged on a circle of paving around a little body of water, with benches conveniently placed to sit and contemplate the pretty scene.

"Shall we sit?" He used his handkerchief to brush dust and

leaves from the nearest bench.

"Look," she said, as she accepted the seat he had cleared for her. "Ducklings!" An adult led a dozen or more little balls of fluff across the water. Rose was counting them out loud and laughing as they swapped places and veered off in different directions, all chirping loudly.

"They will not stay still for me to count them!" she chuckled.

"Eleven?" he suggested, then joined her laughter when two more babies came squeaking from the reeds and merged with the fast-moving duckling ballet around the mother.

Ruadh had been telling himself that he barely knew Rose; that his fascination with her would fade with closer acquaintance. But every meeting so far had him wanting her more. She was kind, intelligent, competent, loyal to her family. He enjoyed being with her. He was used to summing people up on short acquaintance—the skill had stood him in good stead as an officer in the army, particularly as the commander of troops charged with keeping the peace in a hostile land. With Rose, he had passion and the beginnings of friendship.

"Look, Ruadh, this one is coming to see us!" she exclaimed, pointing to a duckling who was attempting to scramble out of the pond just in front of them. "I wish I had something to feed to them."

"The mother is not too happy about the venturer's direction," Ruadh observed as the duck's quacks took on a more urgent tone. His voice was none too steady as he reacted to her use of his personal name. He wanted to hear it again, preferably when they were in bed, her hair spread across his pillow, her voice a husky moan.

The duck didn't want her child too far away, and that raised another objection to a match between himself and Lady Rose. Rose was an Englishwoman and a Southerner. Ruadh's future lay in Scotland, far away from everyone and everything she knew. Ruadh's own mother was English, and she had long missed her family.

In Mama's case, though, she was estranged from her family. Had that not been the case, she could have seen them. Perhaps not often, given the distance, but from time to time. Today, Galloway was not as many days' travel from London as it had been a generation ago. Rose's family could visit, and Ruadh could afford to journey south for a month or so every couple of years, should it come to that.

Rose shook her skirt at the adventurous duckling. "Do as your mother says, until you are a little older," she advised. It tumbled back into the water with a startled, outraged peep and set a straight course for the duck, who sailed off to the other side of the pond, her little flock paddling around her, though several chose to ferry onboard her back. Ruadh's heart did an unusual skip at the sound of her laughter and the sight of her smile.

Even if he did find her attractive, as well as acceptable as his wife, the difference in their ages also worried him. He had at least fifteen years on her, and those fifteen years had been spent at war and in the shadow of war.

On the other hand, while she was young, she appeared to have a good head on her shoulders. The question was, could she cope with his moods, with his sorrow, and the dark energy that gripped him from time to time? He would have to be honest with her before she decided whether to allow him to court her. She would at least know what she was choosing.

So that was it, then. He'd chosen to court her, and it hadn't been a difficult decision at all. He opened his mouth to make a start, but at that moment she turned her head his way, her face alight with laughter, her eyes sparkling. He found himself bridging the gap between them, leaning to meet her and to kiss her. He forced himself to stop, his lips almost touching hers.

"Yes?" he asked. "Or no?"

"Yes," she breathed. It was little more than a whisper, but it was enough. His mouth covered hers, his lips gentle, though the strain on his self-control had his whole body quivering, like an eager horse constrained at the starting line, waiting for the signal.

Her untutored response helped. She was at first passive, then began to return the pressure and movement of his lips. When she parted her own lips, he had his first taste of her. A taste wasn't enough. His eager body wanted him to take more, to delve deep, to clasp her to him and shape her body with his hands, to turn this gentle exploration into an imitation of the act for which his body yearned. Perhaps, in this unexpected haven, even the real thing.

He ignored it, touching her only with his mouth, leaving her free to break their connection if she wished.

She moaned and pressed closer. He began to reach for her but called his hands back under his command. He must end this. Someone could come upon them at any time. He drew away, and at first, she followed, but then she allowed him the distance and sat back, looking adorably flustered.

No time like the present. He had not achieved his rank by dithering about an action once he had decided. "Rose, I have some things I need to tell you before I ask your consent to seek Stancroft's permission for our marriage."

ROSE, STILL LOST in the sensations of Ruadh's kiss, took a moment to understand his words. Then her heart leaped and immediately sunk again. She wanted nothing more than to be Ruadh's bride, but she first needed to tell him about the scandal of her birth.

"I must tell you something too, Ruadh." Better to do it straight away, for once he had heard, that would be the end of it, and he wouldn't have to suffer through telling her whatever he thought was so important. His double identity, she supposed. Of course, if he was considering her as a bride, he would want to tell her that he was the Wolf of Whitecross.

If he told her, she wondered, would it be polite to let him know she was already aware of his alter ego? Or would it be best to let him speak his story and pretend to be shocked and surprised? The only way she could stop him from sharing his information was to speak first and deter him from telling her his identity as the Wolf.

"I would like to speak first," she said, firmly.

"I cannot imagine anything you could say that would change the way I am beginning to feel about you," Ruadh assured her. "But if it is important to you, here I am. I will listen."

I should just blurt it out. "My mother was my Papa's mistress, not his wife," she said. "He installed me in his nursery when my mother died. Peter insists that I bear the family name and am addressed by the courtesy title 'lady', but I have no right to either. I am not a fit mate for a viscount and a future earl, for I am base-born."

Ruadh looked surprised at her first sentence and was frowning by the time she had finished. Her heart sank, but what he said next was not the rejection she expected. "I knew about your parentage, of course. A couple of the ladies I danced with were very keen to pass on the information. I made it clear I cannot abide nasty gossips, and that I would not be asking them for a dance in the future."

Rose gaped. He knew her secret? And yet... he still treated her with courtesy and respect. It was something she'd never experienced from anyone except Peter, her sisters, and their closest friends. It was certainly not something she expected. She found herself quite unable to speak to him. Indeed, her lips were rounded like an 'o'. She blinked and pressed them together. "My lord?" Her voice came out about as strong as the duckling's startled peep.

He took both of her hands in his. "I am sorry people have made you feel you are somehow less than because your parents were not married, but believe me, Rose, it makes no difference to me. If you consent to marry me, I shall count myself the luckiest man in the world. I would be proud to share my surname with you, and to make you a viscountess and later a countess by right of marriage. Let the mean bampots chew on that. And I hope it chokes them."

The two sentences were said with considerable indignation, which made her giggle even as she wondered if he had really thought it through.

"What will your family think, though?" she asked.

"My mother will love you as much as my grandfather already does," he said, promptly. "My father wants only to please my mother. The rest of the clan will follow the lead of their chief." He shrugged. "Such things are less important in Scotland, where we consider every baby as a blessing."

"Can it be so simple?" she wondered. Sincerity shone out of his eyes, but could she really burden him with her flawed self? "I am not sociable like Viv," she warned. "Nor am I as pretty as she."

He kissed her again, saying in between the delicious caresses of his lips and his mouth, "To my eyes, Rose of my life, you are prettier than Viv. I want to uncover every one of your curves and—do things I must not mention until you are mine. Viv is very ornamental, but my heart doesn't leap when I see her. I don't feel the least urge to touch her, to kiss her, to... Well. Enough said."

He drew slightly away again. Not so far he had to release her hands, which he still held, but the distance between them was suddenly more than physical.

"You were brave to tell me what you saw as your flaws, darling Rose. Now let me take my turn. Will you do this for me? Will you listen, and ask any questions you may have, but not make any decision until you have had time to think? Feel free to discuss anything that worries you with your family, if you wish, though I would not like it to go any further. Is that acceptable?"

His eyes searched her face as though Rose's answer would be written there, and perhaps it would, for Viv and Arial had often said she wore her thoughts and feelings in her expressions.

"Yes, of course. None of us gossip, Ruadh. I shall tell you

sometime about how the dowager Lady Ransome, Viv's mother, used gossip to try to destroy Arial. We have a horror at it. What is it you need me to know?" That he was the Wolf? Somehow, she was certain of it.

Ruadh's grip on her hands tightened. "I have several concerns. At first, I told myself I should not court you at all, Rose. But I was too much attracted to stay away. I still see all the objections to the match, though."

"Objections?" Rose asked, when he paused, frowning.

"The age difference, for one. You are not yet twenty. I am thirty-four. I ask myself, would you be better off with a younger man?" His frown deepened. The idea did not please him, which set her heart skipping again.

When Viv had raised the same concern, Rose had considered the matter, and she had her answer ready. "I think age is one of the reasons I have not until now met a single gentleman I could regard as a possible husband. They all seem so young. They do not have a thought in their heads beyond the current fashion and the latest silly wager. Most of the girls Viv and I have met are the same."

To be fair, Viv might appear that way to someone who only saw her outward behavior. "Perhaps they are just pretending to be butterflies without a thought in their heads. Viv certainly is. But I have never been good at pretending. If that is what being young means, I haven't been young since my Papa died." *Which was when my stepmother stopped being secretive and sneaky about her persecution of the unwanted bastard Papa had insisted on keeping.* That was a story she would tell Ruadh another time.

"I do not regard you as old, either, Ruadh." She thought of something else to say. "Do you think you would be happier if you married an older woman? And if so, do you have one in mind?"

That fetched an amused smile. "Do you want me to confess you are the only woman on my mind?" The smile faded. "My home is in Galloway, in Scotland's southwest, far from everyone you have known. If you marry me, Rose, you will be leaving your sisters and your brother behind and going to an unknown country."

Before today, Rose had not believed anyone would wish to marry the Ransome by-blow, so she had not given much thought to leaving her family. It would be a wrench, but surely she could write? And visit? "Women do this all the time," she pointed out. "Unless they marry someone who lives next door, they leave their home and their family and friends, and keep in touch by letter, and with visits?" She made a question of the last few words.

"Yes," he confirmed. "We could have them to visit us, and we can visit them. My family shall love you, Rose, especially my mother. She is also an English woman from the southern counties who married a Scotsman. And she was entirely cut off from her family when she married my father."

Rose sighed. How tragic for them both. It must have been so hard for Ruadh's mother, and also for poor Lord Hardwicke, who had regretted his harshness almost too late.

ROSE WAS WONDERFUL. She didn't dismiss his concerns but addressed them fearlessly and with the common sense he had come to regard as typical of her. But his last and greatest concern about the match was still to come. Perhaps he did not have to tell her. Wasn't he better when he was with her? Calmer. More at ease. Happy, even.

He opened his mouth to say he was broken inside, that he was a seething mass of pain, despair, and anger. What he said instead was, "I am the Wolf of Whitehall."

Rose nodded her satisfaction. "I thought so."

"You knew?" No one else had guessed, he was certain of it.

She smiled at him. "Somehow, I sensed it. I felt it to be true. I kept thinking of you and the Wolf in the same way. And then you said some words as Lord Merrick that I had heard before from the

Wolf. After that, I was nearly sure."

She was so matter of fact about it Ruadh couldn't believe his ears. "You are not afraid?" Ruadh asked. "I go out each night into London and hurt people. Even kill them. I am a violent man, Rose. Not fit to be in company with any woman, let alone a lovely young woman like you."

She regarded him with the patient and slightly exasperated look his mother used to wear when he persisted in saying or doing something stupid. "Ruadh, the people you kill. Can you stop them any other way? Do you kill when you can achieve your goals without dealing death?"

Ruadh felt as if she was speaking an unknown language. "What do you mean?"

In the same patient tone, she said, "When you and I met, you could have stabbed or shot the men who did it. They were unconscious, helpless. It would have been easy to remove them from the world. Easy for a violent man, a killer."

"No," he said, shaking his head. "They were helpless. Killing them would have been wrong."

Her slight smile and her nod indicated she had already guessed he felt this way.

"Very well, I admit I prefer not to kill if I can avoid it. But that does not make me a good man. I have seen things, and done things, that no man should. I am a killer, and you should run from me as fast as you can."

Rose narrowed her eyes as if to see farther into his soul. "Should I be afraid you might kill me?"

He recoiled at the question. "No. Never. How can you think it?"

"I do not," she said. "I know I am safe with you, Ruadh. I am just attempting to understand what it is you think I should run from. You do not kill for killing's sake. You are not a danger to me. What is your concern?"

Ruadh answered without pausing to think, the danger clear in his mind. "I fear I might make you unhappy. I do not sleep well.

My temper is at times uncertain. I suffer from melancholy."

Rose did not answer straight away. With a small crease between her brows, she considered his statements. Then she spoke.

"Do you think I will be more unhappy to be with you when you are sad than to be without you altogether?" she asked. "For if so, I disagree. I have fallen in love with you, Ruadh Douglas, Master of Glencowan, and if you leave me now, I daresay I shall survive, for people do not, on the whole, die of a broken heart. But I will grieve. I will grieve, or so I think, for the remainder of my days."

"You will find someone else," Ruadh protested, but Rose did not agree.

"Never until you noticed me did I catch the interest of a man. Some of them flirted with me as a way to be close to my sister, but I was never the object of any man's desire until you. Nor did a man catch my interest and my attention. Not until you. I very much doubt matters will ever change, so do not console yourself that suitors are lining up and I shall soon find someone better, for there *is* no-one better. Not for me. I have not had, and do not expect to have, another suitor."

What she said lifted his heart, for if she had no other prospects, and if she was as fixed on him as she said, then perhaps she was right. Perhaps, flawed as he was, he was better than nothing.

But Rose had not finished. "Besides. How could anyone possibly be better? You rescued me when I believed I was about to die, or worse. I have seen how you behave with the people that most of Society ignores—the veterans, your grandfather, even the wallflowers at a ball. How you take responsibility for them and try to make their lives better. You are kind and clever and brave, and so handsome it makes my heart ache just to see you. I admire you more than anyone I have ever met. You, Ruadh."

Ruadh lifted his hands and hers with them. He placed a reverent kiss on the back of each hand and another on her lips. "So be it, then. If you are certain you want me, Rose, I shall speak with your brother. I vow to you, I shall be the best husband I can be."

"And I shall be the best wife I can be," Rose replied. He kissed her again for that promise and might have done more if a worried quacking had not broken their absorption with one another. It warned them of the approach, first of a dog, and then of its owner. By then, Ruadh was three paces away from Rose and they were both watching the increasingly frantic fussing of the duck as the dog, a large shaggy beast of indeterminate ancestry, ran to and fro on the bank, loudly inviting the ducks to join him.

His master ran into sight, calling the dog—a boy just out of childhood and not yet at the gangly stage of adolescence. He managed to capture the excited dog and reattach the leash, all the while talking to it. "Bruce, you are in such trouble. How could you? You know you are not allowed to run off without me. I would have brought you to see the ducklings. But I daresay you have frightened them so we will not be able to see them. And Mr. Brown is likely to take us immediately home as a punishment for your disobedience, which you deserve, but I do not. It shall be the kennel outside for you, sir, and mathematics for me."

The dog, hearing only the boy's tone, waved its tail and did its best to lick the boy's face, so the collar was not properly buckled when a tall thin gentleman, quietly and tidily dressed, strolled around the corner from which the boy had emerged.

"Ah, good," this gentleman said. "You have captured our miscreant, Master Harry. Did the malefactor put up much of a battle?"

Master Harry took the inquiry at its face value. "He did not fight at all, Mr. Brown. He likes me."

"A sagacious beast," Mr. Brown declared.

Ruadh and Rose exchanged a smile, and Ruadh offered his lady an arm. "Shall we return to the carriage?" he asked.

They left ducks, dog, and boy behind them, and were soon rolling behind two perfectly-behaved horses, who proceeded at a fast trot around the rest of the circuit of the park and back out into the streets of London.

Stancroft was at home, and willing to give Ruadh an audience in his study. He raised the same concerns Ruadh had, but in the end, left the study and returned with Rose. "You have five minutes while the butler fetches some champagne," he said, "after which I will expect you to join us in the parlor for a celebration."

Ruadh took Rose in his arms, to make the most of the five minutes. He hoped Rose and her family would not want a long betrothal.

Chapter Six

ROSE WAS TOO excited to sleep well that night, and as the sky began to light with the dawn of a new day, she gave up even trying. She moved to the window seat, which was a favorite place of hers. It looked out over the garden, and she could even see much of the mews lane, though not as much as in winter when the trees dropped their leaves.

She enjoyed watching birds in the garden going about their morning rituals and perhaps catching sight of a cat on the prowl, a cart making a delivery to the kitchen from the alley that ran up the side of the house, servants busily shaking carpets, sweeping paths, fetching water, grooming horses, or a myriad of other tasks.

It was too early for any of that now, but within the hour, the mews and the gardens would be bustling with activity. *How lazy we are in comparison to those who serve us. And yet, the work that Peter does, and Arial, too, is essential to the well-being of the nation.*

She would be part of that, soon. As wife to Ruadh, she would have a role in Society. She would care for his house, bear and raise his children, and be his helpmate as he navigated his own position in politics, society, and his family.

The shiver that ran through her was part fear but mostly excitement. A little apprehension was understandable, but she had no real doubts about her fitness for the role in which she had been trained.

As she sat there half-dreaming, her thoughts drifted to the house next door. Ruadh had engaged the private inquiry agents that Peter had recommended. Were they, even now, watching the house?

Perhaps that groom who had just gone inside after sweeping the paving outside of his mews was working for the Wakefields. More probably the peddler who had stopped to sell some item from his tray to a kitchen maid from the house next door on the other side from the Hardwickes. Surely not the boy who was lingering in the mews lane, idly kicking a ball.

The boy ran out of sight. Halfway down the Stancroft garden was a large oak tree in full leaf. It obscured her view of the mews end of the Hardwickes' garden, as well as the back wall and the mews beyond. After a moment, the boy came into view again on the other side of the tree.

Ruadh was planning to visit his grandfather today and bring with him a friend who was a doctor. They were also taking a lawyer, which Mr. Wakefield had suggested. How would that go? Rose could imagine several scenarios, some of them disastrous. What was Lady Hardwicke hoping to achieve? Was it as Viv said? Did she hope to become with child, and to pass the valet's child off as Lord Hardwicke's? In some ways, Viv was more worldly than Rose, who would not have imagined such a thing.

What would Ruadh's mother and father think of Rose? Ruadh had told her a little about them, but his memories were fifteen years old, and what he knew of them today, he knew only from letters.

Her thoughts stuttered to a stop when she saw the Hardwicke carriage pass along the mews lane from the carriage house. It went behind the tree and did not come out. A groom came into sight in the Hardwicke garden, hurrying up to the house and out of her view.

Moments later, half a dozen servants emerged, carrying

trunks, bags, and blankets, on their way from the house to, presumably, the carriage. Rose had to see what was going on behind the tree. She hurried into the first gown her hands could find, slipped her feet into the nearest shoes, and left by way of the servants' stairs.

By the time she reached the door to the garden, the servants next door were carrying Lord Hardwicke outside. She could see him through the trellis and hoped that no one looked her way, for she would be just as visible.

Presumably, they were heading for the coach. She hurried down her own garden path and opened the gate at the end. Yes, they were just taking Lord Hardwicke from his chair, several of them raising his poor weak body to pass him to others inside the carriage.

She looked around for someone who could help, but the lane was currently deserted apart from her and the Hardwicke servants. Except now another carriage had pulled up behind the first, and servants were swarming over both, tying luggage so that it was secure against the jolts of travel.

She took several steps towards the first carriage and called out to the servants. "Stop. Lord Merrick wishes to see his grandfather today."

After a startled moment during which they paused to look at her, the servants turned their faces away and continued what they were doing. Rose hurried forward without any clear idea of how to prevent them from carrying Lord Hardwicke away. "You are assisting in an abduction," she warned the servants "Lord Merrick will…"

A hand fell on her shoulder from behind her. "Really, little bastard. You should not have inserted yourself in our affairs." It was the voice of the valet, Wolfenden.

Before Rose had time to react or even to think, strong hands grasped her by the waist, picked her up, and threw her into the carriage after Lord Hardwicke. The door slammed behind them, and the carriage began to move forward.

RUADH WAS HEADING home after prowling the streets for several hours. He'd left his domino and mask behind in his room, for Wakefield, the private inquiry agent, had given him a warning. At least, so Ruadh had taken it. "The law is a broad brush," the man had said. "We all have a choice about how we paint in the detail. Sometimes, there are people who work within the law to do appalling things. Lady Hardwicke, as Lord Hardwicke's wife, has certain rights. We will have to prove she has acted outside of those rights. Also, on occasion, people work outside the law to do what is just and necessary."

He had then looked straight at Ruadh with his light hazel eyes and added, "Anyone can walk in the rookeries, and if they see a crime or even an act of violence within the law, there's a good chance they will not be arrested for stopping it. But those who go in disguise, cloaked and masked, are likely to be taken for one of the beasts they intend to stop. It would be a pity to see that happen."

On this night, those beasts had decided to take their violence and crime somewhere else. Which was as well, for tonight Ruadh's own violence slept as his heart rejoiced. He didn't want to hit anybody. Not tonight. Perhaps not ever again.

"Mister!" It was a ragged street boy. "Mr. Wolf!" It was the street boy he had saved a couple of weeks ago before he'd met Rose. He had clearly recognized Ruadh even without his domino.

"Call me Red," Ruadh invited.

"Mattie Dinker," the boy told him. "It's the lady. You got to come help the lady." He grabbed Ruadh's hand and pulled. Ruadh went along, a dread pooling in his belly as everything in him clenched at the sudden conviction that 'the lady' was Rose.

The mists from the river had risen with the sun. They cast a glamour over the squalid streets, hiding the sordid detritus of the night, but also providing a masking curtain for those whose desperation might lead them to attack an alert and well-armed man.

For once, Ruadh had reason not to welcome a scuffle that might release some of his energy. He scanned the surroundings as he trotted beside the boy called Mattie, determined not to be taken by surprise.

"Which lady and where are we going?" he asked.

"The lady wot you rescued," Mattie said, impatiently. "The pretty one wot you kissed by the pond," he said.

Ruadh frowned. "Have you been watching me, Mattie?" he asked.

"The lady and you," the boy confirmed. "Wanted to see if'n you could be trusted, didn' I? I figured you'd come back to her house today, so I slept behind her house last night, didn' I. The lady came out of her house to stop some bully boys. They was tryin' to shove an old man into a carriage. Poor old geezer in a big chair wiv wheels. The lady shouted at 'em and they grabbed her an' threw her into the carriage, too. Then the lady and gent from the old man's house come out and both carriages left. I follered them as far as I could, then come for you."

Terror and anger swept through Ruadh, almost felling him, but he forced his suddenly weak legs to continue pumping. They were almost at the clinic. He said, "We'll call in here," and grasped the boy's shoulder to stop him.

"No time, Guv," Mattie insisted, struggling to get free.

"We can't catch up with them on foot," Ruadh explained. "If my friend is here, I can borrow a horse or a vehicle."

It took nearly ten precious minutes, but at the end of that time, Ruadh was on his way with Mattie clinging on behind, and Nate was heading to the Stancrofts to alert them to the problem.

"Which way now?" Ruadh demanded, and Mattie shouted directions as he set the horse into a walk, then allowed it to move faster and faster as the streets grew wider and less crowded.

Too long, too long, the hooves beat out as they cantered along the Strand and then past Carlton House and up St. James Street to

Piccadilly and then Knightsbridge, and still farther. Mattie had somehow managed to follow the carriages until the buildings of the city were left behind and the network of roading choices had reduced to just a few.

"Sorry, mate," Mattie said. "After this, I lost 'em."

But Ruadh knew their direction now. "Mattie," he said, "Would you, by any chance, recognize Lady Rose's brother, the Earl of Stancroft?"

"I reckon so, Red," said the boy. "Big fellow, but not as big as you. Yeller hair. Right pretty. Wife wears a mask."

"Just up ahead I'm going to stop to get a fresh horse. I want you to stay and tell Stancroft where I've gone, and where I think Lady Rose has been taken. Weatherstone Hall in Berkshire, the Hardwicke family seat. I'm going on ahead. Tell the earl I will get Lady Rose out, but I want help to rescue my grandfather."

Mattie looked apprehensive but agreed. It was only after Ruadh was on his way again, having sent a groom with a message to Stancroft and leaving Mattie with enough funds to get himself back to London if needed, that he stopped to think about how the boy must feel, an hour's hard ride from everything he knew.

There was nothing to do about it now. Ruadh's one overriding desire was to get to Rose. He could only hope he had guessed right about where they were taking her.

THE CARRIAGE RATTLED and bounced behind its team for what seemed like hours, though Rose was unable to check the time. Nor could she see the direction they were going, for the doors were locked from the outside, the windows were painted over, and the hatch between the interior and the driver was shut and jammed in some way. It was dark and stuffy, though some light leaked in where the paint was thinner.

Her attempts to attract attention from the driver or another attendant brought no result, and distressed Lord Hardwicke, so she gave up banging on the walls, ceiling, and door and sat with him, holding his hand. She told him that she was to marry Ruadh and that Ruadh would come after them, and he did his best to smile as he nodded his delight at the news.

But she could see the fear and anxiety in his eyes and knew that she was fooling him no more than she was fooling herself.

She consoled herself they could have killed Lord Hardwicke in London if they intended to do him harm. She had no such consolation for herself, though her heart could not believe this was the end. Not now. Not when Ruadh had declared himself and she was about to be married.

Twice, the carriage stopped, presumably to change horses. Rose shouted as loudly as she could and thumped on the door and ceiling, but no one responded. They were off again a few minutes later.

Partway through the trip, Lord Hardwicke became very upset. It took her a minute or two to detect the pungent smell and realize that his bladder had released. In the gloomy light that filtered through the paint on the glass, she found water, soap, and wash clothes in the bag that had been shoved in through the door behind the poor man, and changes of clothes, too. Presumably, the plan had been to give him an attendant, until Rose inserted herself into the situation.

He has one still, Rose decided. She set about making him comfortable, assuring him that she was practically a family member, and that looking after his comfort was a great privilege. The backward-facing seat lifted to show a cavity, and into it, she put the soiled garments, rolled into a ball with the worst of the mess tucked away inside.

The bag also held flasks of liquid, which she opened and tasted. Fruit juice of some kind. She and Lord Hardwicke both had a glass. Rose commented that being kidnapped was thirsty work and thought her patient's eyes showed appreciation at the comment.

At last, the carriage pulled to a stop for the third time, and she heard the sound of a key in the lock. They were opening the door.

"Phew," said one of the footmen Rose had encountered before. "The old duffer has pissed himself. Dirty old geezer."

"One day," Rose told him coldly, "you may be helpless and unable to move. When that day comes, I hope you meet with more kindness than you have shown, for you can hardly meet with less. Lord Hardwicke is clean and freshly changed. You may assist him from the carriage and take him to his room. I shall attend him. Also, arrange for the laundry to be dispatched to the washroom."

The footman gaped at her, standing back out of the way so that Rose was able to insert herself into the doorway. "Have a care," she warned. "He is frail and bruises easily." She held out a hand as if expecting the other footman's help to the ground, and he hastened forward to offer his support.

It was a large manor house, relatively new in construction, set in a neatly kept park. The carriageway ended in a courtyard large enough for a coach and four to execute a complete turn, and they were stopped at the foot of the steps that led up to the front door. A stretcher on legs awaited Lord Hardwicke.

Of the other carriage, there was no sign. Nor were Lady Hardwicke and her lover present. Rose did not know whether they had gone elsewhere, were yet to arrive, or were in the manor but not interested in witnessing the arrival of their two prisoners. She was not going to ask. Time would tell.

"This way, my lady," another footman said, waving towards the steps.

"I will attend Lord Hardwicke," Rose informed him and hurried to catch the poor man's hand just before it banged on the carriage door. He appeared even more frail than before, but the eyes that met hers reminded her of Ruadh—they were the same golden-brown. He looked from her to the servants and glared, stern, proud, and defiant.

She followed as he was carried to the stretcher and helped to make him comfortable. "We will be fine, my lord," she assured him. He smiled as best he could with his twisted lips and squeezed her hand.

She held his hand up the steps, through a large entrance hall, and then up several flights of stairs to a bedchamber. There, she prepared herself for yet another tussle of wills with a man who waited to attend the earl. "I am Lady Rosalind Ransome. You may carry out his personal care," she told him, doing her best to sound as imperious as her friend Lady Snowden at her most lofty. "I shall be with him as a representative of my betrothed, his grandson."

"Yes, my lady," said the attendant, without making a fuss. "If you will excuse me, my lady, I shall make his lordship comfortable."

Rose moved to the window while the attendant did what he needed to do. The room was pleasant enough, but she did not think it was Lord Hardwicke's usual chambers. It was quite small, on the third floor, and had no personal items such as papers, portraits, and books.

From the window, Rose could see the kitchen garden of the manor, which was extensive, and a wide paved path between the house and the garden. A sheer drop separated her from the path and even so, the window had bars on it. The room had probably once been a nursery.

No matter, she could not leave Lord Hardwicke, in any case. At least not until she knew what the man's wife and his valet had in mind for them.

At least she could look after Lord Hardwicke for as long as she was permitted to stay with him. And perhaps she could help whoever came after them, for she had to believe that someone in one of the surrounding buildings had seen her forced into the carriage and that her brother and Ruadh would search for her.

It might take them some time to find her, but they would not quit until she was rescued. Now all she had to do was come up with a plan to alert them they were in the right place when they arrived.

Chapter Seven

R UADH STOPPED AT two inns before he was able to confirm, at the third, that he was on the trail of the carriage in which Rose had been taken away from him. He had been riding for the past thirty minutes with increasing doubt that his initial guess was correct, so what the grooms in the third inn had to say was a great relief.

Not only had they seen a carriage that met the description of the one Mattie had described, but they had all heard the racket that arose from it. Banging, shouting. A woman's voice calling for help. "Oi've been abducted," one of the group screeched in imitation.

The driver and grooms had explained that their master's wife had descended into madness and was being taken home to their manor where she could do herself no harm.

Good for Rose. She had made sure that her rescuers could follow her.

"The lady in the carriage is, in fact, my betrothed," he told the grooms. "She has been abducted, together with my grandfather. I am on my way to retrieve them both, and I want your fastest, most reliable horse." He patted Nate's horse, who had done sterling service. "This fine fellow belongs to the Earl of Lechton. Look after him well, and I will collect him on the way back."

Within ten minutes, he was on his way again, on a horse the stable master assured him could outlast anything else in the stables. He'd broken his fast with a pie and a flagon of light ale, and he knew what inn the carriage he pursued was most likely to stop at next.

"If it's to Weatherstone Hall they're going, my lord," the innkeeper had said, "then the Rose and Thorn is halfway between here and there and is the one the quality use."

Sure enough, they had been there, only ninety minutes before him. Rose had made the same kind of noise and the driver had told the same sorry tale to explain it. Again, Ruadh cajoled out of them the best horse they had, and also directions for the fastest route to Weatherstone Hall.

Perhaps the Countess of Hardwicke and her accomplice had taken a different route or changed horses at different inns on this route, for nobody he questioned had seen either of them. However, the inns on this route were very busy. The carriage was much like any other, and if the countess did not insist on her title, she might not have been noticed.

The valet, with his pale coloring, was more noticeable. Perhaps he had stayed in the carriage. Perhaps they were taking their time and Ruadh had passed them along the way. He wouldn't see them on this route, which was fit only for a rider, but that didn't matter. What was important was getting to Rose and his grandfather.

Only when he knew what he was up against could he make a plan to bring them safely away. He would claim to be sketching, he decided. That would give him a reason to ask about local sights, including local great houses, and would mean he could loiter without people wondering at his presence.

He stopped in a town just a couple of miles from Weatherstone Hall to change horses again. He'd need to leave the new horse at the inn in the village near the manor, and he wanted no rumor of a long-distance traveler from London to reach the ears of Lady Hardwicke and her lover.

He had been in the saddle for five hours when he reached the village. He'd ridden past the gates of the manor just five minutes down the road, and every fiber of his being demanded that he storm the place there and then, but he stuck to the plan: Set up a cover story. Return surreptitiously to Weatherstone Hall. See if he could find out where his beloved was being held. Count the number of servants and investigate the lay of the land.

After that, he could decide whether to act on his own, approach the local magistrate, wait for Stancroft, or something else.

He paid for a room for the night and stabling for his horse. "I may stay one night or several," he told the innkeeper, a cheerful woman in her middle years. "I fancy sketching hereabouts. Indeed, I must away this minute, for I saw such a pretty bridge on my way into the village that I nearly stopped straight away. But I lose track of time when I am sketching, and the poor horse, you know. I thought it best to stable the beast. I shall be back for dinner, I expect."

The innkeeper commented that the bridge down by the manor was right pretty and that dinner would be a nice leg of lamb, and perhaps a fish pie.

Ruadh was already sauntering away as she sent her good wishes after him. As soon as he was out of sight of the inn, he slipped into the nearby field and ran in the shelter of the hedgerow until he reached the manor walls.

They were easy to climb, and the woods on the other side ranged to within a hundred yards of the back of the house. He stopped on the edge of the woods to decide his next move. He could see the stable yards off to one side, where horses were being released from a carriage—not the one he had been chasing, which had yellow wheels, so presumably, it was the one that had brought Lady Hardwicke and Wolfenden here.

Something white flapped on the third level of the house and caught his eye. He narrowed his eyes to sharpen his vision. A large patch of cloth. A sheet, perhaps? And on it, a shape, a pink outline. He had to get closer to confirm what his eyes were telling him, but he was almost certain the shape was a rose—an English rose, with four petals. His clever Rose was signaling her location.

AFTER THE LONG journey, his sponge bath, and half a bowl of broth, Lord Hardwicke slept. The attendant brought Rose fresh water to refresh herself and a plate of bread, cheese, and fruit—berries, which Rose realized could be used to make a sign for whoever came looking for her.

"Is there anything else you need, Lady Rosalind," the attendant asked.

Rose was anxious for him to go, so she could make her sign. "Nothing at the moment."

"Please ring the bell, my lady, if you think of anything," said the attendant.

As soon as the door shut behind him, she spread a spare white sheet out on the floor and squashed berries into it in the shape of a rose, four petals, and a circle of dots in the center to represent the stamen and pistils.

She shut the window on the sheet, which flapped and should attract attention. Unwanted attention perhaps, but here at the back of the house, perhaps it would remain in place long enough to be seen by those who were coming to her rescue.

After that, she had nothing to do but wait, but it could not have been more than ten or fifteen minutes before there was a knock on the door. The attendant had returned with a footman who said he was here to escort her to Lady Hardwicke.

Rose briefly contemplated refusing, but he was much bigger and brawnier than her. Her dignity would be better served by pretending she was responding to a polite invitation. She asked the attendant to look after Lord Hardwicke, and sailed out of the room past the footman, keeping the poker she had purloined from the fireplace hidden in her skirts.

"Which floor?" she demanded.

They were in the drawing room—both Lady Hardwicke and Wolfenden, standing on the other side of the room by a side table. Rose entered at the end of an argument, which they stopped when they realized they had an audience.

"…never have brought her," Lady Hardwicke was saying.

"She would have raised the alarm. Better to get rid of her here, away from discovery." That was Wolfenden.

"We can't…"

We can't what? Lady Hardwicke had realized that Rose and the footman had arrived, and stopped speaking, leaving Rose to wonder whether Lady Hardwicke was against killing her or whether she had some other objection to Wolfenden's plan.

"Lady Rosalind," Lady Hardwicke said.

Rose gave an abbreviated curtsey. "Lady Hardwicke." She decided to take the initiative. "Lord Hardwicke would benefit from my calendula and honey ointment. Unfortunately, I left too suddenly to collect the pots I had ready, but if your tenants can supply honey and the calendula flower heads, I will make some more. It is best if the flowers are slowly steeped in oil, but I can produce an effective balm without doing so."

The two villains were gaping at her.

Best to keep talking. If she assumed she was here for their convenience, they might go along with it. "You brought me here, I assume, to nurse his lordship, and I am willing, but I will need supplies."

That shook them from their surprise, but not in a good way. Lady Hardwicke complained, "Lord Hardwicke has a nurse, and does not need a silly girl." At the same time, Wolfenden growled, "You inserted your nose where it was not wanted, and I brought you here to silence you. Permanently."

Inside, Rose quailed. She scorned letting her fear show. "Do you think for a moment that your abduction of me was not observed? From one of the houses, or from the mews? I daresay my brother is on his way even as we speak."

Since they had been at a ball the night before, she would not have been missed until late morning, and it was now mid-afternoon. She did not have much hope of Peter finding her trail immediately, or even today, though she knew he would not give up, and neither would Ruadh. "My betrothed will be with him, I expect. I am to marry Lord Merrick."

"I think not, little bastard," said Wolfenden. He reached behind him, and when his hand appeared again, it held a dueling pistol, which must have been on the table. "You will be buried in the woods long before they figure out where you have gone."

Rose felt her head spin and the voices of her abductors appeared to come from a long way away. She could not faint! Lord Hardwicke needed her. She would not faint! She stiffened her weak knees and prepared to throw herself out of the way as soon as Wolfenden's eyes showed he was about to shoot. She would see his intent in his eyes, would she not? The heroine always did in Viv's horrid novels.

"Wolf, darling," said Lady Hardwicke. "Surely there is another way."

"We are so close, Yvonne," the valet told her. "We have sacrificed so much, and we are on the brink of success. You and I and the child will have it all. We cannot stop now. She could have us hanged, my love. She must die."

Lady Hardwicke looked at Rose and then at her lover. "I do not like it. I wish you had not pushed her into the carriage."

He made an impatient sound. "We must deal with what is, not with what we would like," he told her. "She is here, and she is a mortal danger to you and to the child."

Rose did not expect the next voice that joined the conversation. Now her knees did almost give out, and she had to grip the edge of the closest table for support.

"Not, however, as mortal a danger as I am," said the newcomer.

Ruadh! He must have entered from the window, for he stood just inside the room, his pistol trained on Wolfenden. "It has two bullets," he told the valet. "I can shoot you and your paramour without reloading."

"But can you shoot me before I shoot Lady Rosalind?" sneered Wolfenden. Still, his voice shook, and so did his hand. His forehead suddenly glistened with sweat and his eyes had gone wild.

Ruadh, by contrast, was rock steady.

Not so Rose, whose stomach felt as if it was about to return her last meal. But as she squeezed her hands into fists she felt the poker that she still held. Time to change the rules of the game. She threw the poker at Wolfenden and flung herself sideways.

The poker landed with a clang that was almost drowned out by the bark of two pistols—Wolfenden had flinched as he pulled the trigger, and his bullet flew into the ceiling. Ruadh did not flinch.

Lady Hardwicke screamed and dropped to her knees beside her lover. Ruadh held his pistol steadily on the pair of them, but his other arm was open until Rose ran into it, to be held tightly to his side.

"He is dead! You have murdered him," Lady Hardwicke lamented.

Two menservants hurried into the room and stopped short at the sight of their mistress weeping over the dead body of their master's valet, while Ruadh stood with a smoking pistol aimed at them both.

"I AM LORD Merrick, Lord Hardwicke's grandson," Ruadh told them. "I have come to rescue my betrothed, who was kidnapped by Lady Hardwicke. Lord Stancroft, my soon-to-be brother-in-law, will be here soon with the magistrate. Until then, I want Lady Hardwicke watched at all times. She is not permitted to leave this room." The footmen stared at him for a moment, cast a glance at Lady Hardwicke, who was weeping over Wolfenden, and then chorused, "Yes, my lord."

"If you can fetch the pokers, my love," said Ruadh, "I shall secure the guns and make sure there are no more in the room. Then we can check on my grandfather."

"He was asleep when I left him a few minutes ago, Ruadh," Rose told him, as she collected herself and then the poker from upstairs and all the fire irons in the decorative holder by the drawing-room fire. "The attendant with him appears to be kind and competent."

Ruadh had found the pair to the pistol Wolfenden had used. "There are no more weapons," he confirmed.

He gestured to the door and Rose led the way out of the room. "Lord Hardwicke is in the old nursery," she told him. "This way."

Ruadh followed her past several gaping servants and up the stairs, but as soon as they were on the nursery floor, he swept her into his arms. "I was so frightened for you," he admitted.

"I knew you would come for me," Rose told him. "I am glad you came so quickly, for Wolfenden gave me a few worried moments." She was understating the case, for Ruadh could feel her quivering in his arms and her heart still pounded from the fear of Wolfenden's threats. Ruadh held her closer.

His mouth descended on hers and his hands pressed her against his body. He was breathless and shaking with need when he withdrew his mouth enough to speak. "I thought I had lost you," he declared. "I hope you do not want a long betrothal, Rosalind Ransome, for I cannot bear to be parted from you."

"As soon as you like," Rose told him, which warranted another kiss, even deeper and more wild than the last.

"This week, if I can manage it," Ruadh decided.

Rose was alive and well and in his arms, and that was all Ruadh wanted to concern himself with. But they still had his grandfather to look after, a houseful of servants of questionable loyalties to handle, a wicked step-grandmother—was that an appropriate thing to call her when the woman was no more than his age?—to deal with, and a magistrate to find.

In short, he could not take his caresses and hers where he dearly wished he could. Back to duty. "Let us go and check on my grandfather. We have a murderess countess to deal with and a wedding to arrange." Indeed, his bride-to-be was pink and tousled, and he had to look elsewhere or he would lose all sense of place and time.

"Which room is my grandfather in," he asked.

He was pleased to see that, as a result of his kisses, she had to blink several times and give her head a swift little shake before she could answer the question. "This way, Ruadh."

The old man was still asleep. The attendant sat near the head of his bed, quietly reading, but stood when they entered the room. Ruadh introduced himself, keeping his voice down so as not to disturb his grandfather.

"I am Merrick, Lord Hardwicke's grandson, and I am taking over responsibility for his care. Once he has rested, I intend to take him back to London, and from there, by easy stages to Scotland. My betrothed, Lady Rosalind, here, tells me she has found you kind and competent. I would be pleased if you continued to care for him as long as he is here, and longer if it pleases you."

"Lady Rosalind is very generous to say so," the attendant said. "May I ask the reason for the change? The butler appointed me, but I was told his instructions came from Lady Hardwicke, and that Lord Hardwicke would be remaining here."

"Lady Hardwicke does not have my grandfather's best interests at heart," Ruadh said, harshly.

The attendant looked uncertain, and well he might. He had only Ruadh's word for what must seem an arbitrary change in plans. But before Ruadh could say anything more, he was interrupted by a thunderous knocking on the door two stories below, followed by a voice Ruadh recognized, shouting Rosalind's name.

"Peter," Rose said even as Ruadh commented, "Stancroft."

"Your brother made better time than I expected," Ruadh commented.

Sure enough, Stancroft had arrived, with several friends and more than a dozen retainers. Also, it transpired, the local magistrate. The man was determined to keep an open mind, even after Ruadh explained the circumstances under which he had shot Wolfenden. "I will need to listen to Lady Hardwicke's side of the story, my lords," he insisted.

But the footmen had disobeyed Ruadh's instruction and allowed Lady Hardwicke to retreat to her bedchamber. When they went up to Lady Hardwicke's room her door was locked on the inside, and when they broke down the dressing room door, they found her dead on her floor, an open vial labeled *prussic acid* on the table next to an empty glass. There was no note.

Since the magistrate insisted on them staying until after the coroner's inquiry into the deaths, Stancroft took Rose off to order rooms at the nearby inn. Ruadh wanted to howl, to bay like a wolf in protest at the separation, but Stancroft had the right of it. She couldn't stay here with him.

At least, if her backward glance meant what he thought it did, she felt as torn apart as he did. Ruadh needed to talk to Stancroft about that fast wedding.

A short time later, he walked down to the village to join Rose and her brother for dinner at the inn. A constable stood guard over the two bodies. Lord Hardwicke and his attendant were guarded by one of the servants Stancroft had brought with him, and Ruadh was not needed until the inquest in the morning.

There was a fourth at dinner. Stancroft's friends had returned to London, but David Wakefield, the inquiry agent, had remained. "I have some information that may be relevant to the inquest," he told Ruadh. "Lady Hardwicke and her lover were overconfident. Most of the servants in the townhouse heard them talking to one another and to your grandfather, and some were willing to give evidence. Of course, it won't be necessary, now.

But I will be able to tell the coroner that they intended to keep Lord Hardwicke helpless, while hiding his condition from the outside world, until such time as they had a son they could pass off as Lord Hardwicke's."

"Wolfenden kept insisting I must be killed because I was a threat to Lady Hardwicke and the child," Rose commented. "Do you suppose she *was* with child?" She was visibly distressed at the thought. "Why on earth did they leave London, and take me?"

"They thought he was isolated, and easy prey, Lady Rosalind," Wakefield commented. "Your friendship with him must have been maddening. When Lord Merrick turned up, their whole scheme threatened to become unraveled. Removing Lord Hardwicke from London was an act of desperation. Kidnapping you and bringing you along was stupid. Neither Stancroft nor Merrick was going to accept you had simply disappeared."

Ruadh exchanged a nod of agreement with Stancroft. Wakefield had that right.

"As it happened," Stancroft told Rose, "Lady Macclesfield, in the house next door to the Hardwickes, saw you being abducted. Apparently, she thought it was a maid misbehaving, and went back to her ablutions. But after she was dressed, she had convinced herself that the maid was unwilling and decided it was her civic duty to make inquiries, so she sent a footman along the row to ask if anyone was missing a maid. When we realized you were missing, Arial went straight along to ask exactly what she had seen."

"I was in the Hardwicke kitchen, talking to the servants," Wakefield said, "pursuing my inquiries. So, when the Macclesfield footman arrived, I already knew that Lady Hardwicke and Wolfenden had left early, by carriage, taking Lord Hardwicke in another carriage. I went next door to ask Stancroft if he knew who the maid might be and found him sending messengers to his friends to set up a rescue party."

"Then your lad arrived, Merrick, with confirmation they were heading in this direction. We can't have been much behind you, but from the sound of things, that half hour might have made all the difference to Rose." Stancroft shuddered, and so did Rose.

Ruadh wondered how to raise the topic of an early wedding. In the end, Stancroft did it for him, as they were sitting over a last glass of wine at the end of the meal. "Rose tells me you plan to go home to Galloway as soon as possible and take your grandfather with you," he said. "What do you intend to do about your betrothal?"

Direct and honest. Ruadh liked it. "Marry Rose by license, if she is willing and with your consent," he replied. "I do not want to leave her, Stancroft."

"Rose?" Stancroft asked.

Rose's answer was in her starry eyes and the smile that spread across her face, but she gave the words anyway. "Yes, Ruadh. I will marry you. As soon as it can be arranged."

Stancroft nodded. "Good. There's no way to stop the Macclesfield woman from talking, but at least we can make it clear that Rose was kidnapped by a pair of wicked would-be murderers and rescued by her betrothed, who by the time we tell her story will be her husband. It will be a nine-days' wonder and long over when next you come to London. It won't hurt Rose's reputation and it may enhance Vivienne's, since she may be supposed to have inside information about the whole adventure, so she will be invited everywhere."

Rose chuckled. "Which Viv will like, and I would hate."

When dinner was over, Stancroft and Wakefield left the happy couple alone in the private parlor for ten minutes, and after that, Ruadh walked back to his grandfather's estate at charity with the world.

At the inquest the following morning, Ruadh and Rose both gave evidence and so did Wakefield. The coroner questioned the carriage driver and grooms, who supported Rose's account, though they claimed they believed Rose to be the lunatic Wolfenden had claimed.

The only new facts came from the doctor, who was able to confirm that Lady Hardwicke had not been pregnant and that she had taken hydrocyanic cyanide, more commonly known as prussic acid. Ruadh supposed the woman had been lying to her lover as well as everyone else.

The jurors did not take long to return the expected verdicts. Wolfenden had been shot to prevent him from killing Lady Rosalind Ransome and in self-defense, and Lady Hardwicke had poisoned herself.

Wakefield returned to London after the inquest, with messages that he promised to deliver to the Hardwicke household and to Stancroft's countess. Ruadh, Rose, Stancroft, and Lord Hardwicke left the next day and traveled by easy stages back to London, giving Lord Hardwicke a break from the carriage at each change of horses.

Ruadh had offered the attendant who had been looking after Lord Hardwicke a bonus for continuing in the role until they were at home in Galloway, and he was able to appoint someone permanent for the position. For Ruadh had asked Lord Hardwicke if he indeed wished to come home with him and Rose, and the old man had tearfully agreed.

It was evening by the time the carriages pulled up in front of the Stancroft townhouse, and before long they were all being welcomed back, even Ruadh receiving a warm hug from Lady Stancroft and Lady Vivienne, and an enthusiastic handshake from Miss Turner.

Lord Hardwicke stayed to meet them all, and then his attendant and one of the footmen carried him up to the room that had been prepared for him. "Thank you for having him to stay, my lady," Ruadh said to Arial. "I am reluctant to trust Lady Hardwicke's servants with his care. I have already fired the footmen and grooms who helped to abduct Rose, and I'll be interviewing the rest of them tomorrow, to see who can be trusted. It might be that we need a clean sweep, but since my grandfather is coming to Galloway with me and Rose, I only need a caretaker staff next door."

"Call me Arial," said the lady. "You will be my brother before the end of the week. Wakefield dropped off the common license this evening, so now it is only a matter of booking the church at a time to suit the vicar."

"And I'm Viv, and he's Peter and she's Pauline," said Lady Vivienne, pointing to her brother and then her stepsister. "Now tell us what happened. Peter's letter was very frustrating. 'Rose is safe and so is Lord Hardwicke. Lady Hardwicke and Wolfenden are both dead. Lord Merrick and Rose are to be married.' That is not a story. It's a laundry list."

Peter laughed, but he agreed. "Rose, you should start, since you were in it first."

They took turns to tell their parts of it, until Ruadh ended with, "I suppose we will never know what set them fleeing. I suppose they realized I was not fooled by Wolfenden's little masquerade and thought I might give up if they were gone. Taking Rose made certain I would never give up, however."

They discussed it a little further, but really, there was nothing to add.

As Arial said, "It is all very sad, but now it is over, and we have a wedding to look forward to."

Epilogue

ROSE WAS NORMALLY slow to wake fully. Which was a polite way to say she was as cross as a bear until she had had a cup of tea and something to eat. Early in their marriage, Ruadh had discovered one other thing that put her in a good mood first thing in the morning—morning intimacies woke her up in the most delightful of ways.

For the last two months, however, she had been unable to do anything active first thing in the morning without reaching for the clean chamber pot that was kept for the purpose. Ruadh's husbandly duty had changed from giving her as many orgasms as he could manage to ringing the bell for a cup of tea and a slice of dry toast while she lay as still as possible.

If that cure for an upset stomach did not work, he held himself responsible for keeping her hair out of her way while she heaved over the chamber pot.

Mama assured them both that morning sickness seldom lasted beyond the middle of the third month, which would be some time in the next few weeks, and certainly, the tea and toast were generally enough to settle her digestive system enough for her to cautiously get out of bed.

Today she lay obediently flat while he rang the bell, then allowed him to help her up so he could place a couple of pillows behind her, propping her up enough to drink the tea when it arrived.

The kitchen would have a kettle on the hob, the toast cut, and her teapot warming, so her maid would be here with her tea tray soon. The whole house knew that the Master's lady was with child, and went out of their way to make sure she was cherished.

Ruadh climbed carefully back onto the bed, taking care not to rock the mattress, and settled with his arm around her. She rested her head on his shoulder and he kissed the top of her head. The sound she made in response was more like a growl than not, which made him smile. Who would have guessed that the woman who had brought sunshine into his darkness would be such a grump in the mornings?

At the knock on the door, he called, "Come in." It could only be the maid. She knew not to enter without an invitation, and no one else would be at their door at this time of the morning.

A few minutes—and half a cup of weak black tea and half a slice of toast later—Rose spoke for the first time. "Good morning," she said.

"It is at that," he agreed.

And it was. Every morning waking up with Rose was a good morning. Even on the nights that the nightmares hounded him, he had only to reach out and touch Rose and she grounded him in the present. Or, if he was lost in the dream, her voice would bring him back, her love warming the depths of his soul and soothing his pain.

Work helped, too. There was plenty of it. The previous Earl of Glencowan had favored his privileges over his duties and Ruadh's two cousins had been interested only in spending their allowances to the maximum, not in cherishing the people dependent on the estate and the family. Ruadh's father and mother needed the help of Ruadh and Rose to undo years of mismanagement, disdain, and neglect.

Even so, they had greeted Ruadh's hospital project with approval, and each allocated time to help first with seeking the support of their peers and later with practical advice and assistance. The facility would be opening in Glasgow in April.

"Do you think they will be here today?" Rose asked.

Rose's sisters were coming to spend Christmas with her. Not Peter and Arial. Arial was close to being confined with her next child, and could not make the long journey, but Vivienne and Pauline would be here in the coming days.

"If not today, then tomorrow or the next day," Ruadh told her.

She had managed the rest of the cup and the slice of toast, and—he leaned his head forward to check—had not turned any shade of green. "Are you ready for your bath?" he asked her. Maggie, the maid, had left the door to the adjoining room open a crack when she went through after stoking the fire, and he had heard the footmen filling the bath while Rose was eating.

She met his lips with her own. "You are so good to me, Ruadh."

"I love you," he told her.

"I love you."

He would never tire of hearing her say it.

RUADH RODE OUT after breakfast to check on one of the tenants who had been ill. Rose and her mother-in-law met with Mrs. McGregor, the housekeeper, to ensure that all the plans were in place for the coming festivities. The Glencowan household celebrated both the English Christmas and the Scots Hogmanay, but the previous earl and his sons had usually been away at house parties during the season, and besides, the new Countess of Glencowan had her own family traditions that she wished to incorporate.

"And you, Rose, dear," she asked. "Is there anything we can add from your own family celebrations?"

Rose suggested a special recipe she had begged from the cook before she left and wondered if Mama would consider adding red and gold ribbons to the swags and wreaths of Christmas greenery.

Arial had been a wonderful older sister, but Rose had never experienced a mother's loving care until she met Mama. Mama had taken her into her arms and into her heart from the day she and Ruadh arrived at Lannock Castle. Father, too. Though Rose missed her English family, she had found a new family here in Scotland.

And soon, Vivienne and Pauline would arrive. Perhaps even today!

After the meeting with Mrs. McGregor, Rose and Mama spent an hour with Grandfather Hardwicke. He was much improved—Ruadh's friend Nate had said that his condition was worse than it should be because he had been malnourished, and prescribed plenty of good food.

It had worked to the degree that Grandfather now had the use of the right side of his body, though his speech was still slow and sometimes hard to understand. The Glencowans had made a couple of rooms on the ground floor into a bedroom and parlor for him, where he could be pushed into the great hall or the drawing room to join the rest of the family, and where new French doors had been installed so that his attendant could take him in his chair straight out onto the terrace.

Not in this chill, though. He was sitting by the fire playing chess with the attendant who had come with them from Weatherstone Hall, but he gestured for the attendant to carry the board away when the ladies entered. "How are my daughter and granddaughter today," he asked, as he did every morning, rejoicing in the pair of them, and added, as he had since Ruadh and Rose had shared their news, "And how is my great grandson?"

They caught him up on their good health and on the preparations for Christmas. A maid arrived with refreshments, and they enjoyed a cup of tea together until Rose saw out the window that a rider was approaching along the carriageway. "Ruadh is home," she said. "Would you excuse me, Mama, Grandfather?"

With their blessing, she hurried to the front hall, arriving just as Ruadh entered. His face lit up and, heedless of the butler, he held out his arms. She hurried into them for his kiss.

"I have news to make you smile, my love," he told her.

"The Quigs are well again?"

"Better." His grin showed he was delighted at whatever it was.

"Then tell me…" she demanded.

"I passed a carriage on my way through the village and had the pleasure of greeting your sisters. They had stopped because one of the horses had thrown a shoe, but the inn was putting a new one into the traces as we spoke. They will be about ten minutes behind me."

Rose had to hug the man again. "How wonderful. Oh, how shall I wait ten minutes? I must tell Mama. And Mrs. McGregor! I must tell Mrs. McGregor."

In fact, the ten minutes flew as she rushed from person to person, and it seemed like no time before she was weeping all over her sisters' shoulders, which alarmed them, rather, until she explained, "Do not mind me. I am with child and Mama says that breeding women often cry at the least thing. And here is Mama!"

She proudly introduced her sisters to Lady Glencowan, and then to Lord Glencowan, who had emerged from his study to meet them.

Finally, she led them off upstairs to their bedroom, where Vivienne whispered to her, "The castle is not nearly as wild as I expected, and nor is Galloway."

"It is not as tame as our part of England," Rose admitted, "but I like the wild."

Especially the kind of wild that was Ruadh Douglas. Master of Glencowan and of her heart.

THE END

Author's Note

I hope you have enjoyed this story, which was inspired by *Little Red Riding Hood*. If you have not yet read other stories in the series, *Lady Beast's Bridegroom* (inspired by *Beauty and the Beast*) tells Peter and Arial's story, and *Perchance the Dream* (inspired by *Sleeping Beauty*) explains what befalls Vivienne and Pauline on their way home from their visit to Galloway.

There was no Scots regiment known as the Reds, but it is true that serving soldiers in the Highland Regiments had a dispensation from the laws against wearing the kilt. In any case, the ban was lifted in 1784, some forty years before this story.

It is also true that Scots regiments were amongst those sent to Ireland at the end of the Napoleonic Wars. They were far more sympathetic to the Irish than the British regiments on the same duty, and areas where the Scots were quartered were generally more peaceful than elsewhere. Even so, being representatives of a hated invader is not an easy duty. A number of incidents inspired Ruadh's misery in my depiction of his character.

ABOUT THE AUTHOR

Have you ever wanted something so much you were afraid to even try? That was Jude ten years ago.

For as long as she can remember, she's wanted to be a novelist. She even started dozens of stories, over the years.

But life kept getting in the way. A seriously ill child who required years of therapy; a rising mortgage that led to a full-time job; six children, her own chronic illness... the writing took a back seat.

As the years passed, the fear grew. If she didn't put her stories out there in the market, she wouldn't risk making a fool of herself. She could keep the dream alive if she never put it to the test.

Then her mother died. That great lady had waited her whole life to read a novel of Jude's, and now it would never happen.

So Jude faced her fear and changed it—told everyone she knew she was writing a novel. Now she'd make a fool of herself for certain if she didn't finish.

Her first book came out to excellent reviews in December 2014, and the rest is history. Many books, lots of positive reviews, and a few awards later, she feels foolish for not starting earlier.

Jude write historical fiction with a large helping of romance, a splash of Regency, and a twist of suspense. She then tries to figure out how to slot the story into a genre category. She's mad keen on history, enjoys what happens to people in the crucible of a passionate relationship, and loves to use a good mystery and some real danger as mechanisms to torture her characters.

Dip your toe into her world with one of her lunch-time reads collections or a novella, or dive into a novel. And let her know what you think.

Website and blog:
judeknightauthor.com

Subscribe to newsletter:
judeknightauthor.com/newsletter

Bookshop:
judeknight.selz.com

Facebook:
facebook.com/JudeKnightAuthor

Twitter:
twitter.com/JudeKnightBooks

Pinterest:
nz.pinterest.com/jknight1033

Bookbub:
bookbub.com/profile/jude-knight

Books + Main Bites:
bookandmainbites.com/JudeKnightAuthor

Amazon author page:
amazon.com/Jude-Knight/e/B00RG3SG7I

Goodreads:
goodreads.com/author/show/8603586.Jude_Knight

LinkedIn:
linkedin.com/in/jude-knight-465557166

www.ingramcontent.com/pod-product-compliance
Lightning Source LLC
Chambersburg PA
CBHW070354310726
48977CB00002B/440